TROUBLE AT THE NEW DAWN B & B

A Cottonwood Springs Cozy Mystery - Book 8

BY

DIANNE HARMAN

Published by: Dianne Harman
www.dianneharman.com

Interior, cover design and website by
Vivek Rajan

ISBN: 9781704598079

CONTENTS

ACKNOWLEDGMENTS

Many years ago my husband and I went up to the Mt. Shasta area in Northern California for a vacation — him to fish, me to do whatever. We stayed at a lovely B & B, and while my husband was fishing, the owner of the B & B and I became friends.

He was a delightful person, and since I love to cook, we spent time in his large kitchen making breakfast casseroles for the guests, and he even gave me a personal tour of the area in his jeep.

However, my favorite memory of the trip was his large, very large, German Shepherd dog who instantly took to me and adopted me as one of his people. One day I mentioned that I was going for a walk and the owner told me to take the dog, whose name I've forgotten, with me.

The owner said that some of the people who lived down the different trails around the B & B lived there because they wanted to get away from people and didn't take kindly to visitors. He mentioned that his dog would stop me from going down those trails. And believe me, he did.

When I approached a trail that the dog decided was off limits to me, he'd move in front of me and block my way, completely. Once I tried to move around him to see what he'd do. Same thing. There was simply no way I was going down that trail on his watch!

I've thought about that B & B a lot over the years and always regarded my stay there fondly, thinking how lucky I was that we chose that particular one from its website on the internet.

If for some reason we hadn't, what a treasure I would have missed. Thus, Trouble at the New Dawn B & B was born. What a shame it would be if that B & B couldn't open.

So to the B & B in Shasta, the owner, and the dog, although your names have been forgotten, my time there certainly has not. Thanks!

And to my readers, to those of you who work so hard to get my books to see the light of day, and to Tom, thank you!

Win FREE Paperbacks every week!

Go to www.dianneharman.com/freepaperback.html and get your FREE copies of Dianne's books and favorite recipes immediately by signing up for her newsletter.

Once you've signed up for her newsletter you're eligible to win three paperbacks. One lucky winner is picked every week. Hurry before the offer ends!

PROLOGUE

It had not been a good day. It seemed like everything had snowballed downhill until their mind was ready to explode. Actually, it was probably one of the worst days they'd had in a long time.

Just as soon as they'd think things were starting to turn around for them, something would happen that took the wind right out of their sails. What they really needed was a break, because dreaming about getting away from their problems wasn't working. They needed something more. A way to blow off some steam and have some kind of a new experience that would make them feel better.

The seasons were starting to change, so they decided to go outside to try and clear their head. Maybe a bit of fresh air would help. They grabbed a jacket, stepped out onto the front porch, and shut the door quietly behind them. The sun was tucked behind the trees, casting everything in long shadows that stretched into unnatural shapes. Walking across the wooden porch and over to the steps, their footsteps echoed in the space beneath the porch and the ground below. When they got to the steps they slowly sat down on the top step.

A soft breeze rustled through the trees as a car drove by. They inhaled deeply, closed their eyes, and tried to push the stressful thoughts away. They attempted to shift their focus from their problems to the pleasant sounds of nature surrounding them, but the distraction wasn't working. Their frustrations followed them. No matter how many ways they tried to relax, nothing worked. Not today.

They knew that looking at what was going on in their neighborhood probably wasn't going to help them, but they sat there just a little longer watching the activities in the neighborhood, hoping it might have a calming effect on their jangled nerves.

When they saw a little girl go riding down the sidewalk on her bicycle, they were envious of how carefree she looked. Her hair was flying back from her face and her cute little cheeks were all puffed up because of her wide grin. She looked completely happy just pedaling away on her bicycle, not even thinking she was probably old enough to ride her bike without the training wheels.

I can't remember a time like that, they mused as they started to walk back to the door that led inside. *A time when I didn't worry so much.* They looked at the door, dreading going back into their house. They knew no one else was there, but they still didn't want to go back inside. It was as if the walls themselves were soaked in stress, but there was nothing else for them to do unless they wanted to stay out on the porch.

When they were back in their house, they sat down at their computer and decided to scroll through social media. Maybe that would help silence the troubling thoughts that continued to rumble around in their mind. It was a way they could get away from their problems, at least for a little while.

They started scrolling, but it didn't take long before a familiar ad popped up. The ad featured the new bed and breakfast that was coming to Cottonwood Springs. It had a nice photo of the place and spoke about how they were gearing up for their grand opening. The New Dawn B & B would be accepting reservations soon. In order to be one of the first to reserve a room, they suggested following them on social media or joining their mailing list.

They scoffed. They'd already heard enough about this new B & B to last them a lifetime. To a certain extent, they realized that their irritation at the new B & B was misplaced anger from everything else that was going wrong in their life, but even so, they couldn't shake it. Soon, they found themselves clicking on the link and navigating to the site. Not that they hadn't already looked at it numerous times before.

The website was informative and well put together. It had a dark green background with white lettering and featured another image of the place. It promised a date that reservations would start being taken and featured a countdown timer. Having a bit of experience with websites, they recognized the platform that had been used to build the website. This piqued their curiosity and caused them to navigate to what they suspected would be the page that allowed the admins of the site to log in.

As the sun set, the room around them grew dark and the laptop screen was the only light in the room. Their face was illuminated by the greenish glow given off by the computer screen. Their eyebrows were pulled together in intense concentration as they clicked and fumbled around the site.

At some point they decided they wanted to hack the website and take it down. They'd been thinking about how to do it for some time. It was hard to say what exactly had spurred their motivation to do it this time. It could have been boredom, jealousy, or even a little bit of curiosity just to see if they could do it. They'd never before tried to get into someone else's website.

It took a bit of time and patience, but eventually, they found their way in. It was somewhat of a shock when the login page disappeared and the back end of it all was displayed. Smiling, they started poking around to see what was there. Whoever had built it was clearly talented and knew exactly what they were doing. It was laid out beautifully. There were only a handful of pages that were currently live, and each thing was labeled so if someone else was to take the site over, it would be easy for them to find their way around.

After a few minutes they found the pages that would go live once the website officially launched. Those were the pages that nobody else had seen yet. The whole thing was very clean and well organized. There was a place for people to make a reservation online and even pay for their room ahead of time.

Snippets of code here and there linked the website with the booking software that had been installed and was all ready to go. The whole thing had been done in an extremely professional manner, and they didn't doubt that the New Dawn B & B would become a popular place for people to stay.

That last thought really made them mad. They couldn't place their finger on why, only that it did. But their anger didn't have to make sense. Especially not when they were already having a terrible day to begin with. Actually, if they really thought about it, they couldn't even remember the last time they felt as though they'd had a good day. Just that thought alone propelled them onward.

As they continued to look at the site, they began to get an idea. They realized the website wasn't the cause of their problems, but it seemed to be there whenever they were feeling down and depressed. Maybe if they took out the website it would make them feel better. Anyway, it was something to take their frustrations out on, a way to feel like they had some sort of control over the world around them.

They found the section that showed who had access to the site and they changed the password to the login that they'd used. Now they would be the only one who could get in. Next, they skipped over to where all the pages for the site were and unpublished each and every one of them. Opening a new tab, they tested their handiwork to see if the website was truly gone. When they typed in the web address, they were met with a page saying that there was nothing there. Satisfied, they smiled and closed their browser.

Maybe they were taking it out on the owners of the New Dawn B & B or the designer of the website, but they didn't care. Sometimes the only thing you can do with anger is to pass it on so that it will leave you alone. They realized that although they didn't feel completely better, at least they'd done something about it.

CHAPTER ONE

"Do you think I'm odd, just because I want all this lead-up to the opening of our new B & B to be over?" Brigid asked as she flopped down on the couch beside Holly. She was hot and tired, glad to be away from the next door house for a while, so she could take a break.

The house in question was formerly Linc's home, but after marrying Brigid and moving into her home, they decided to convert Linc's house into a B & B. Linc had kept her busy all morning doing things at the B & B and she was more than ready to sit down and relax. Her hair was pulled back with a bandana, and her shorts and tee shirt were covered in sweat and grime, but she was determined to make sure she was there to help him, every step of the way.

"No, I think it's perfectly understandable," Holly said as she turned to face Brigid. "You guys have been working like crazy to get things set up over there. Did you finally get all of the furniture moved around?"

"I certainly hope so," Brigid said. She draped her arm across her eyes as she sighed deeply. "Linc keeps changing his mind. I know he just wants everything to be perfect, but I think he's going to drive me crazy before he finally makes up his mind.

"I just want to sit and watch some TV or do something relaxing. I'm afraid if I go back over there, he's going to want to change it all back again." Brigid hadn't realized when Linc asked her to go over to the house this morning and help him move a few things, just what his definition of "a few" had been. It seemed as soon as he moved a couple of things, he wanted to move even more.

"What do you mean, switch it all back again?" Holly asked. She was still in her pajama shorts and tee shirt that she'd slept in. It was a weekday but there was no school, and she was doing her best to take advantage of it. She didn't want to get up any earlier than she had to. School had been a little more challenging lately, and all she wanted was to take it easy today. Her dog Lucky was curled up next to her, his little body tucked beside her leg as if he needed to touch her for comfort.

"By the way, Brigid, I made some white chocolate macadamia nut muffins when I got up this morning. Let me get you one. It might make you feel better."

A moment later Holly returned from the kitchen and handed Brigid a muffin. Brigid took a bite and said, "Thank you. That is absolutely delicious. I think it will help keep me sane."

"My pleasure. Now what happened?" Holly asked.

"We started by moving everything we'd moved last night. You know how we spent all that time yesterday moving things around?" Brigid asked. And they had. Yesterday they'd rearranged everything until Linc thought it was perfect. Not one piece of furniture had been left untouched. When they'd come home last night, she was sure it had been the last time she'd have to move any furniture for a while.

"Of course. You guys were really working hard when I checked on you when I got home," Holly nodded. "I couldn't believe Linc was still at it yesterday." She'd gotten her hair trimmed and a loose strand of hair fell from her messy bun on top of her head and hung around her face. She sighed and tucked it behind her ear. "Remind me to never get a haircut again," she grumbled.

Brigid smiled. She understood where Holly was coming from, but she thought the change was nice. She was tempted to tell Holly, but she shook her head and continued. "Apparently last night when Linc was in bed, he couldn't get to sleep and he started thinking about what we'd done. Long story short, he wasn't happy with it. He woke up wanting to move almost everything back to how it had been before we'd moved it."

Brigid pulled her arm away from her eyes and turned toward Holly. "I swear, if he makes me do this again, I'm going to pay Wade to help him."

"Tell him it looks great and to stop worrying," Holly suggested. "You know he's just overthinking it all. He has a bad habit of doing that when he's worried. He really wants this B & B to be a big deal, so even the slightest thing like where a chair should be placed is going to have him overanalyzing it for days."

"I know," Brigid said, her eyes going wide. "I tried telling him it looks good just the way it is, but I think he believes I'm just saying that so we won't move it anymore." She was starting to get a little frustrated with him.

"Aren't you?" Holly chuckled.

Brigid grinned and gave her a knowing look. "Partially, but the furniture looks good either way. I really don't see what difference it makes if we check them in on the left side of the table or the right side. He's thinking way too hard about this, and he won't listen to me."

She'd been doing her best to come up with some way to convince him it was fine the way it was, but so far, she hadn't had any luck. The best she could come up with was to play along and pray that at some point, he'd be satisfied.

"I'll go talk to him," Holly said as she stood up. "Maybe since I've been busy with work and school and not over there helping, he'll take my word for it. Besides, by now he must be getting tired of it, too. Maybe a little nudge in the right direction will get him to relax about it."

"Don't let him rope you into moving anything," Brigid warned. "He's a smooth talker. Before you know it, your day of lazing around will be gone and you'll have rearranged most of the house." She was teasing of course, but she also didn't want all of Holly's plans for her free day to go out the window.

Holly laughed. "I'll do my best." She quickly changed clothes, slipped out the back door, and headed across the yard to the B & B.

Brigid sighed and settled back farther into the couch. She really hoped Holly would be able to get Linc to relax. They'd been working so hard on the B & B for so long, she didn't know when they last had a night out. She'd been dreaming of going out to dinner at a restaurant and maybe catching a movie afterward. Actually, she wouldn't mind if they just got a pizza delivered and sat down to watch something on TV.

As long as it didn't have anything to do with the B & B, she'd be happy. It seemed like it was a lifetime ago when their conversations didn't revolve around paint colors and couch placement. Brigid hadn't ever thought she'd hear her husband worry about what curtains matched which paint colors. She closed her eyes and nestled her head into the couch cushions. Maybe she could just close her eyes for a little while…

The sound of her phone ringing made Brigid jump. She could feel the lingering feeling of a nap tugging at her brain. "So help me, if this is you Linc, I'm not going to answer the call," she said as she picked up her phone. When she saw it was her sister, Fiona, she sat up and answered it.

"Hey, Fiona," she said as she answered. "What's up?"

"You aren't super busy, are you?" she asked. "If you are, you can forget I called. I'm sure you guys have a lot going on right now."

"Trust me, I would welcome a distraction," Brigid sighed. "Please, give me a good one." Even going to her sister's house would be a welcome escape at this point.

Fiona laughed. "Having that much fun are you, huh? Okay, well I was wondering if you and Holly were free later today. I've been working on a few designs, and I need some opinions."

Brigid remembered that her sister had decided to take a step back from the bookstore she owned and start designing her own line of clothes, something she'd always dreamed of doing. She was incredibly proud of Fiona for making such a dramatic decision, and she enjoyed seeing what new designs she'd created whenever she got a chance.

"Sure, that would be fun," Brigid said with a smile. "I'd love to see what you've come up with."

"Good," Fiona said. "Don't set your hopes too high. Some of the stuff may not be all that great. I really don't know at this point. Just make sure you both wear something that's easy to change out of."

"What are you saying?" Brigid asked.

"I may have made things to fit you two," Fiona said carefully. "If you don't like them, you certainly don't have to wear them. But I'm going to need models, and I thought if you two don't mind…"

Brigid wasn't so sure about being a model, but she had no problem trying things on. "If it helps you out, I'll do whatever needs doing," she said. But she made a mental note to keep an eye out for her sister trying to snap a picture. That was where she drew the line.

"I really appreciate it, Brigid. I know you have a lot on your plate right now."

"Happy to do it. When do you want us?" Brigid asked.

"Anytime," Fiona said quickly. "I'll be home all day. I'm letting the new hires at the bookstore get their feet wet on their own today. They shouldn't be overly busy."

"Who else did you end up hiring?" Brigid asked. "I know you hired Levi, but you never told me about anyone else."

"She's new in town," Fiona explained. "I'll have to introduce you to her later. She's one of a kind, which makes her a perfect fit for the store."

"Sounds interesting," Brigid said. "I'll talk to Holly when she gets back from next door, and we'll figure out a time to come over."

"Okay, see you later," Fiona said as she ended the call.

Brigid was a little leery about being a model for her sister, but she didn't want to damper her sister's enthusiasm. She wasn't exactly the same size that she used to be, and what if the clothes didn't fit her very well? Fiona had always been a bit thinner than she was, and she'd always had the ability to look great no matter what she was wearing. Everything seemed to flatter her figure.

Brigid was afraid that all of Fiona's clothes would end up making her look like a balloon with pants or worse. But she had faith in her sister. If Fiona had kept her in mind, maybe it wouldn't be so bad.

Settling into the couch, Brigid allowed her shoulders to relax as her head tilted back and her eyes started to close. There was still no sign of Holly, and a nap sounded like a really good idea. She knew if she stayed on the couch, she'd surely get woken up when Holly came back in. Forcing herself to open her eyes, she stood up slowly from the couch.

Her body groaned at having done so much and then being still for too long. She kept her eye on the window, looking for Holly, as she hobbled toward the hallway. Maybe if she laid down on the bed for just a little while, she'd feel a little more on her toes than she did at that moment.

Making it to her room, she shut the door behind her, and spread out on the bed. She had just long enough to think about how comfortable she felt before she dropped off to sleep.

CHAPTER TWO

Nora Russo had just finished preparing breakfast for her lone guest at her B & B. She'd opened the B & B almost six months ago and still felt like she didn't know what she was doing. Of course, she'd followed most of the advice she'd found online, but even so, things just didn't seem to be working out the way she'd hoped they would. Her guest had left for the day, leaving Nora to clean up and tackle her list of things to do.

When she'd finished washing the breakfast dishes, she headed to the bathroom to get ready for the day. Even though she'd hurriedly gotten dressed earlier that morning so she'd be presentable for her guest, it wasn't anything she'd wear outside the B & B. She ran a brush through her hair before putting it back up into a ponytail. She washed her face and paused to look at herself.

Nora was in her late 30's and still single. She'd hoped that opening her own B & B would allow her to finally feel satisfied with herself. Granted, she was the only one in the town of New Haven, Colorado to have a B & B, but it didn't seem like her idea was going to give her the life she'd been hoping for. However, she was crossing her fingers that soon she'd have more than one guest at a time. Once that happened, she'd feel a little more comfortable with how her B & B was doing. Right now, it all seemed like the luck of the draw.

She finished up in the bathroom and walked to her bedroom. She found a pair of black knit pants with a loose vee neck t-shirt, and put them on. Next, she pulled on her shoes and socks before heading to her office to take care of some bookwork. Her office wasn't a big room, but it was all that she needed, big enough for a desk and a filing cabinet. Nora left the door open, just in case someone happened to drop in. She was always ready for an unexpected guest.

As she did the bookwork, she saw that her finances were starting to improve. Last month had been tough, but thankfully the guests were starting to come to the B & B with a little more regularity. She hoped that the trend would continue and bring her even more guests next month. She could really use a win, especially considering how much her parents hadn't approved of her decision to open a B & B.

They'd always wanted her to go to college and get some sort of fancy degree, but that had never been what she wanted to do. She could remember them telling her from the time she was a little girl that they'd started a savings account for her. They had told her she could either use it for school or something else if she chose. Nora had let the money sit in the account while she debated what path she wanted to take.

Eventually, Nora had opted to open a B & B and had spent most of the money in the savings account to buy it and do a bit of remodeling. After that, she planned to use the rest of the money to stay afloat while she waited for her business to improve. She was still doing okay, but what she really wanted to do was start putting money back into the account, rather than taking it out.

Nora decided to do some more research on how to make her B & B more profitable. Maybe she could find more places to advertise for free or find someone she could barter services with. Perhaps there was another B & B that would share ad space with her or something like that. So many places suggested becoming friendly with the local sites or other B & B's for referrals, but Nora had never been an overly friendly person to begin with.

Even though approaching others wasn't one of her strong suits, she decided that maybe today she could get up the courage to send out an email or two. She could test the waters before she gave up on the idea entirely. After all, there had to be a reason it was suggested. That's when she saw the ad for New Dawn B & B.

The photo of the New Dawn B & B showed a beautiful home that appeared to be rustic and modern all at the same time. There were neatly trimmed evergreen bushes out in front and a curved sidewalk. She couldn't help but click on the link to see where this place was located. The photos made the place look comfortable and inviting, like an old friend's home that you hadn't seen in years, welcoming you with open arms.

She assumed that maybe it was in Montana or Idaho. It reminded her of somewhere beautiful and yet cold. The photos showed what looked like mountains in the distance, so it had to be somewhere like that. As the page loaded, she was surprised to see it was located in Cottonwood Springs.

"That's only about thirty minutes away from here," Nora muttered to herself. The website said that they weren't taking reservations yet, but that people could sign up to be on their mailing list in order to be the first to book one.

"I don't even have a mailing list," she said with a pout. She'd never even considered that. She grabbed a note pad and made herself a note to look into it. *Maybe I should keep looking around so that I can see what else they're doing,* she thought to herself.

As she clicked through the site, she realized this place meant business. The website looked professionally done and the photos of the place were outstanding. They had to have hired a professional photographer to get such unique and flattering photos of every single room. The picture of each room had been taken from multiple angles, so you knew exactly what everything looked like before you even showed up.

It was a great idea and one she intended to use on her website. She wondered how many people had already clicked on the site and started planning a trip so they could stay at the New Dawn B & B when it opened. If she had just run across the site and was looking for somewhere to spend a weekend, she knew she'd be enticed to go there. That was when she clicked and found a photo of the owners.

They were a beautiful couple with a very pretty teenage daughter. Two dogs sat happily at their feet. They looked like the type of people who always got what they wanted, kind of the All-American family. The couple had probably been high school sweethearts. Gazing into their happy faces, Nora had to admit that even she would want to stay with them. How could she ever compete with them and their site? In comparison, she looked a bit like some crazy cat lady, minus the cats, and her site couldn't even begin to compare with theirs.

As Nora scrolled through and looked at the rest of the photos, a sinking feeling settled over her. Even though she'd been doing alright, she knew that once this new place was open, there was no way she could compete with them. Her B & B was nice, and she'd put a lot of time and effort into it, but she was fairly sure her newness showed. She was also aware that she could be a bit scattered, so she wasn't sure that she'd always be the type of hostess she wished she could be.

She stood up and closed the window, trying to put the new B & B over in Cottonwood Springs out of her mind. Maybe they were far enough away that they wouldn't affect her business, such that it was. She stood there for a while, looking out the window. She decided she needed some fresh air. Maybe a little manual labor would help take her mind off of the New Dawn's perfect little family and perfect B & B.

She walked out to the back porch, grabbing her gloves and a rake. There were still dead leaves that needed to be cleaned up. Maybe when she was finished raking, she'd feel better about her situation.

Usually, she would have thought the day was beautiful, but she was still too preoccupied with her thoughts to even notice. What had first started out as shock mixed in with a little resentment had turned to anger.

"Why do they have to be so perfect?" she grumbled to herself. "Perfect house, perfect relationship, and perfect family." She was aware that she didn't really know anything about the family who owned the New Dawn B & B, but that didn't stop her from assuming.

"That stupid ad and their gorgeous website," she continued. "It was so good they even had me convinced, and I'm not even looking for somewhere to stay!"

She aggressively raked the leaves out from under the trees and bushes, making quick work of it in her flustered state. Even a few sticks came flying out as she kept working.

"I can't have another place opening up so close to me," she finally decided. "That could be the end of my B & B." Her mind kept running in a loop about the website, as if it was taunting her. "Maybe there is something I can do about it," she said, thinking out loud.

Nora didn't have the first clue what to do, but that didn't mean she couldn't figure it out. She was resourceful and intelligent, and she knew you could find about anything on the internet these days.

While she continued her raking, she started to think about her idea. If she could manage to get the website taken down or even just get the ad taken off of the internet, maybe it would be enough to buy her some time. Once she had a bit of a following, she was certain she'd be okay.

What she really wanted were loyal guests who would keep returning to her B & B. Nora didn't have many expenses. As long as she could cover them and make a little money, she'd be fine, but she didn't see how that was going to happen as long as a great-looking B & B like the New Dawn was going to open up so close to her B & B.

Continuing her yard work, she thought about what she could do to knock the New Dawn B & B off the internet, well, at least until she was a little more successful. That should be enough to give her a fighting chance. After all, this was simply business.

Nora felt a pang of guilt when she thought about the friendly faces of the family, but she couldn't let her emotions get in the way. Emotions wouldn't save her business. She had to do what was needed to stay afloat. Anyway, they looked like they had enough money to manage on their own. What difference would six months mean to them? And to her, it might mean everything.

She nodded to herself, rationalizing her decision. Now all she had to do was finish the yard work and then head to the store. After all, she had a B & B to run.

CHAPTER THREE

"I can't wait to see what else she's made," Holly said excitedly as she rode with Brigid toward Fiona's house.

"She's already made a couple of things for you, and I think they've looked great on you," Brigid said. One of them was a blouse that had really brought out Holly's eyes. It was almost the exact shade of them, and the cut of the blouse had looked great on Holly. Brigid smiled at her as she turned down Fiona's street. As soon as she'd told Holly that Fiona had some clothes for them to check out, she'd been ready to go.

"Thanks," Holly said as she returned the smile. "I really think she should start looking into selling her designs. I'm not sure how, but I feel like she could really be successful if she gets her designs out there. She's got a lot of great ideas that I think people would love."

"I agree, but I'm not sure in today's world if anyone would be willing to wait for custom clothing," Brigid said with a sigh. "I mean, think about how long it could take her to make something."

"Are you kidding?" Holly asked, shocked. "People would be lining up to wait. There are tons of people out there who would think it was the best thing ever. Even if she just started sharing her designs online, and not necessarily selling them, she could get some serious buzz going."

"I admit I don't know much about the online retail world," Brigid said. "Granted, I know how to shop online and do all the normal stuff, but how people make money by just being themselves is beyond me."

"She could do it," Holly said confidently as they pulled into Fiona's driveway. Holly noticed that Brandon's car wasn't there. "Looks like Brandon must be at work."

"He works hard to keep the ski lodge running," Brigid said as she turned off the engine. "Maybe if Fiona can pull this clothing thing off, he could pull back a little."

"Maybe," Holly said as she unbuckled her seat belt. "But you know he works hard just for her. He's the type who would have to be talked into relaxing." They got out of the car and walked towards the sidewalk.

"I think they both really deserve it," Holly continued. "Maybe they could leave little Aiden with us and they could go on a vacation." They were on the front porch and Brigid turned to Holly as she knocked on the door.

"We could definitely do that for them. Aiden likes coming over, and there are a ton of things we could do to keep him occupied. He might have a tough time at night, though. Let's keep it in mind."

The door opened and Fiona grinned at them. "Hello, ladies. Come on in," she said. She stepped back from the door as she motioned for them to come in.

"Why do you look like the cat that ate the canary?" Brigid asked her. She'd learned a long time ago that when Fiona smiled like that, it meant she had a plan. Brigid was always a little up in the air whether or not she'd be okay with what Fiona had up her sleeve. "Why are you smiling like that?" Brigid asked. "It makes me nervous."

"No big deal," Fiona said with a shrug "But I did get a free reading from one of Melanie's friends."

"Oh?" Brigid asked, surprised as she followed her sister into the living room and the three of them sat down. "How did that come about?" It sounded like something she would have heard about if it had been planned in advance.

"Well, Melanie has started this online business where she helps people get more in touch with their intuition. She has this one person she's been working with for a while now, and she feels this woman has a real gift. She wanted to give the woman some practice and asked me to be her guinea pig," Fiona explained as they sat on the couch.

"It sounds like it went well," Brigid said. She'd always liked Fiona's friend, Melanie. Brigid had never really believed in psychics before she'd met Melanie, but she had used her gift to help Brigid more than once, and she didn't doubt her anymore. Not when some of Melanie's dreams had helped Brigid with cases she'd worked on with the sheriff's department. Granted, she couldn't use what Melanie told her as evidence, but it sure had saved her a lot of time.

"It did. She told me I needed to have more faith in myself," Fiona said as Holly interrupted her.

"Which is exactly what we've been telling you," she said in a sing-song voice. She winked at Fiona when she looked over at her.

"Oh hush," she said with a chuckle as she lightly slapped Holly's knee. "She also said that I am a natural with business and branding, so she felt that my clothing business was going to prosper."

"Big deal. I could have told you that," Holly said as she rolled her eyes.

"Yeah, yeah," Fiona said as she, too, rolled her eyes. "But she also picked up on our parents," she said as she locked eyes with Brigid.

Brigid grew silent as Fiona looked at her. Brigid knew her sister was watching her carefully to see how she reacted. Holly looked from one to the other. "I've never heard anything about your parents," she said softly.

"I don't talk about it much," Brigid admitted. "Not that I don't want to. It's just…"

"It's hard to talk about?" Holly offered. "You don't have to say anything…"

"Brigid, you don't have to worry. I know you feel bad…," Fiona began.

"Well of course I do," she said quickly. "Can you blame me?"

"Not at all," Fiona said shaking her head quickly. "But you lived far away. It's not like you could just pop over and see her."

Holly continued to look at them as they spoke, trying to piece together the conversation. Finally, Brigid turned towards her and began to explain.

"As you know, I lived in Los Angeles before I moved back to Cottonwood Springs," she began. "You also know that I grew up here and my parents lived here. One morning my mom was rushed to the hospital because she was having trouble with her vision. Dad took her to the emergency room, and they found out she had a massive tumor on her brain."

"Oh, wow," Holly said softly.

Brigid felt her hands begin to shake, so she took a deep breath and released it to steady herself.

"It was already fairly big, and the doctor referred her to a doctor in Denver. But the tumor was aggressive, and she ended up back in the hospital a couple of days later. I was trying to figure out how to juggle work and my husband at the time so I could come back here. My dad kept trying to convince me that I was worrying for nothing, but I could feel it in my gut.

"I was doing everything I could to get back here. But when Mom was rushed to the hospital, she didn't make it through the night. They had put her in an ambulance to go to Denver and Dad was going to join her in the morning. He couldn't forgive himself for not riding in the ambulance with her. By the time I finally got back here, his heart had given out, and we were planning two funerals." Brigid swiped angrily at the tears that had started sliding down her cheeks.

"Oh, Brigid," Holly said softly. "I'm so sorry." Her eyes became watery as Brigid looked away. This was another reason Brigid wasn't a fan of talking about any of that. It stirred up things she'd rather leave alone. She felt since you can't change the past, why dwell on it?

"Brigid has always blamed herself for not being here," Fiona said to Holly. Brigid dried her tears and looked at her sister.

"Of course I have," Brigid said quickly. "Maybe I would have noticed that something was wrong with Dad," she said irritably.

"But you wouldn't have," Fiona said, shaking her head. "And that's what this woman told me. She explained that the bond between Mom and Dad was so close, it was supposed to be this way. This woman knew all of it without me telling her anything. She said Mom was insistent that I tell you that you have to be easier on yourself."

"I know I do," Brigid sighed as she sniffled. Fiona grabbed a tissue from a nearby box and handed it to her sister. "It's just easier said than done." She couldn't fight the rogue tear that slid down her cheek. As she swallowed, a lump formed in her throat that was painful and hard to get rid of. It was as if it had grown in an instant, threatening to cut off her air.

"I'm sure it is," Fiona said sympathetically. "We can talk more about what she said later. Besides, you'll be meeting the woman."

"I will?" Brigid asked, surprised. She was grateful for the distraction and being able to think of something else.

"Because, funny enough, the woman recently moved to

Cottonwood Springs. She's the person I hired to work at the bookstore," Fiona explained. She seemed unsure how Brigid would react to this revelation.

"You hired a psychic to work at the store?" Holly said excitedly. "Are you freaking serious?" She looked like she was about ready to jump out of her seat.

"Yep, I guess she's a psychic medium and an energy healer. Although I don't know much about all of that. I got the general idea that's what she is because I've read a lot of books about that kind of stuff, but I don't know how she specifically does it. I figured that was a conversation for another time."

Brigid wasn't sure what to think about Holly's excitement. Granted, she knew there were legit psychics in this world as Melanie had proven, but that didn't mean she wanted someone filling Holly's head with a bunch of nonsense. "I see," she said simply. She trusted Fiona's judgement, but she still wanted to meet this woman and decide for herself if she'd trust her.

"Don't worry, Brigid, she's also a Christian. I'm telling you, we had the most fascinating conversation afterwards about Jesus and God. She said some things that really made sense, you know?"

It was obvious Fiona found the woman interesting, which was a plus. Fiona was a good judge of character and whenever she found someone interesting, they tended to be good people with a lot of depth to them. Still, what if this woman was just good at tricking people?

Brigid didn't want to get in an argument with her sister, so she said, "Let's talk about these clothes you made…"

"Oh! Yes!" Fiona said quickly as she stood up from where she was sitting. "Just wait until you see them. I'll check on Aiden real fast to make sure he's still sleeping, and then I'll bring them out." She hurried down the hall, leaving Brigid to wonder what her sister was getting into.

CHAPTER FOUR

Jack Hubbard enjoyed being self-employed and working for himself. It gave him the freedom to work when and where he wanted. He was free to take a vacation whenever he wanted or just take a day or two off once in a while. But it also had some serious drawbacks, the biggest one of which was finding clients.

It seemed like every time he turned around there was another ad on television about how easy it was for people to build their own websites. They made it seem like everything he'd spent years learning was pointless and that anyone could do it. Granted, those drag and drop builders were pretty enticing, but they still didn't create a one-of-a-kind web page like he could. Knowing how to write a unique code and create something from it was still amazing to him. No drag and drop builder could do anything like that.

That was why Jack had decided to go into this line of work. It straddled the line between creativity and real-world practicality. It gave him a way to express himself, and at the same time, have something tangible that was produced as a result of his effort. It was fun taking a client's ideas and bringing them to life. Creating a fully functioning website while typing in bits of code was like pulling something out of thin air and then molding it with your hands. It was pure magic to him.

Jack sat down in front of the TV with an egg salad sandwich and some cheese crackers. His mother had won prizes at the county fair for her egg salad and the first thing he'd done when he left home was get her recipe. He still felt that was one of the best decisions he'd ever made.

He'd learned a long time ago to never eat in front of his computer, and anyway, it was better for his eyes. After he had to replace a keyboard because he accidentally dropped a can of coke on it, he made it a practice to keep food out of his office. Another big plus was getting to unwind for a short time and think about something else. That seemed to help his creativity more than anything else.

After eating his lunch and watching an episode of his favorite show, he went back to his home office. It was probably the most comfortable room in the house. Since he spent so much time there, he'd decided to make it a room where he'd be comfortable spending large amounts of time.

He'd bought a desk with an attached bookshelf so he could keep his reference books close at hand. It was tucked in the corner with a lamp nearby so he could easily read whatever reference book he was using. There was no way he could keep every snippet of code locked away in his brain forever.

This way he could easily look up what he needed whenever a situation came up and he couldn't recall something. He'd attached a stereo to his computer so he could have some soft background music. A marker board hung on a nearby wall so he could make notes of an idea or remind himself that a bill needed to be paid. He felt like he'd created the perfect office.

Jack felt fortunate that he could live wherever he wanted. When his grandparents had passed away, Jack's parents offered him their house on the edge of Cottonwood Springs. It made the uncertainty of his work a little more stable. He could live rent free there, and as long as he could pay his utilities and eat, he was relatively secure.

Plus, moving somewhere a little more rural seemed to have helped him save a little money. There wasn't much to do in Cottonwood

Springs and even fewer places to eat out, so he wasn't particularly as tempted to spend what little extra money he had on entertainment or eating out.

Sitting down at his computer, he opened his email to see if there were any messages from prospective clients. There was one, a small business owner in New Haven who wanted to know how much he charged to set up a website. He knew from experience that wasn't a good sign.

If someone was concerned with the cost of setting it up right out of the gate, that meant they were probably on a very tight budget. Even so, he typed up a reply to her and sent it off. Mentally he crossed his fingers, hoping he was wrong, and she'd be his next client. Sometimes people surprised him. Maybe he'd get lucky, and she'd end up not only being a client, but a big one.

Seeing that there was nothing else but spam and newsletters, he pulled up the list of people who had contacted him recently. He'd found that if he followed up with people, it could be the nudge they needed to become a client. Often they were just on the fence and a simple phone call to check in with them or a quick email could pull them back in.

There were two that had emailed him recently, so he typed up a quick message letting them know he was just touching base once more to find out if they still needed his services. The last one had been an inquiry over the phone.

He'd been quite surprised that he'd gotten a call from someone here in town for a website. Apparently the old sheriff, Rich Jennings, had referred a guy named Linc Olsen to Jack. Linc was opening a B & B and wanted to set up a website to get the word out.

The photos were the main thing about B & B websites. When Jack had talked to Linc, he'd given him a quote and suggested that he hire a professional photographer to take photos.

Jack had told him after that was done, he'd be able to build a site for the B & B. He decided a quick phone call to Linc would probably be enough to bring him in as a new client. After all, why wouldn't he hire someone local? Someone who was nearby, available for any questions he might have, and also available if Linc wanted to have face to face meetings.

Picking up the phone, he carefully dialed the number he'd written down before leaning back in his chair. After a few rings he heard a man answer.

"Hello?" It sounded like a man, but he wasn't sure if it was the same person he'd spoken to before.

"Hi, this is Jack Hubbard. I was calling for Linc," he said politely.

"This is Linc," the man on the other end of the line said.

"Hey Linc, I was just touching base with you to see if you still needed that website built?" he asked, using his most cheerful voice. "I spoke to you about it previously in reference to your new B & B. Congrats on that, by the way. I wish you all kinds of success."

"Thanks, but I'm sorry. I won't be needing your services. My, uh, daughter actually built it for us. She's only sixteen, but she did an excellent job. I was fairly surprised, not that I didn't believe in her or anything. I guess I just didn't realize she'd knock it out of the park the way she did. She really portrayed the New Dawn B & B in a great way."

"I see," Jack said, doing his best to not sound too disappointed. "Well, I'm happy if you're happy. Good luck with the new business," he said before he ended the call.

He couldn't believe it. He'd lost a client to some kid. He opened up a new page online so he could search for the website she'd done. He'd bet it was extremely basic and not very professional looking. He was sure Linc would be back when he realized he'd made a mistake by having his daughter do it.

He found the link to the site and clicked on it. What appeared on his screen was not at all what he'd been expecting. Instead of the bland site he thought he'd see, it was a beautifully laid out site that did the place some serious justice. Linc must have taken his advice to hire a professional photographer for the photos because they were artistic and very well done.

Jack was afraid his version of the website wouldn't have looked as good. It pained him to even think that, but it was the truth. He wondered just how a sixteen-year-old could do this, because this website put some of his work to shame.

"Darn," he said aloud as he leaned back. If it was true that a high school kid built this, he was in trouble. The site even had a newsletter form for people to sign up so that they'd be notified when the B & B started taking reservations. There was a slideshow of all the photos for the B & B as well as a nice page showing the family and their dogs.

If that young girl in the family photo is Linc's daughter, Jack thought, *she must really be good and she's only sixteen.*

"This is completely unacceptable," he said shaking his head. "What if people find out this site was built by a kid? If only there had been some problems with it," he said as he clicked through all of the links. Everything worked seamlessly. "Too bad it wasn't junk."

If it had been, he could have used it to help his business. He would have shown it to people as a reason why you want to hire a professional. Instead, it seemed to do the opposite. It was almost the poster child for a DIY website.

Why would someone pay him when they could do it themselves? he thought with a sinking feeling in his stomach.

That's when an idea hit him. What if he could get into the site and mess it up? Maybe he could ruin the code it was using or do something else to ruin it. Linc would probably hire him to fix it, and Jack would look pretty good. After all, if word got out that this girl could make websites that well, what was to stop other people from going to her?

He found where credit had been given to the photographer, someone named Levi Andersen. Jack was curious. He'd never heard of this person and wondered if maybe he was an up and coming local. Whoever this Levi was, his photos were great, and Jack thought about hiring him when he had a project that needed photos.

Good photographs could really make or break a website. You can design the best-looking site, but if the photos were lousy, so was the site. Opening yet another search tab, he entered Levi's name. Having professional connections was always a good idea.

It took a while to dig through the results, but he finally found a Levi Anderson on social media who lived in Cottonwood Springs. Jack figured that had to be the person, and clicked on the link. When he realized that Levi was a teenager, he felt his stomach drop to his feet. Two kids, working together, had managed to make an absolute stellar website. Just great. They were the poster children for NOT hiring pros to do it for you.

Jack closed his browser and turned away from his computer. That was it. He had to do something. There was no way he could let kids take over his business and force him back into a regular job. He had no choice. He was going to have to do something about this. That beautiful website needed to get ugly and it needed to get ugly fast.

But could he really bring himself to do that? To completely trash such a great looking site? He wasn't sure, but something had to be done. He couldn't wait around for something to happen. Jack knew he didn't have a choice. He had to take care of the situation and he had to do it right now.

CHAPTER FIVE

Brigid stood before Holly and Fiona wearing the final outfit her sister had made for her. The neckline of the blouse was wide, exposing her collarbone, and it was made of a soft grey fabric. There was an adorable bow in the same material off to the side. The pants matched in a flattering style that made her feel confident. She felt as though she was well-dressed, but not overly so.

"Oh, that is so cute on you!" Holly gushed. "You have to wear that on a date with Linc. He'd love it!" She was so excited, she started to clap.

"You think?" Brigid asked as she spread her hands down her side. She looked down at her outfit and smiled.

"Turn around, I want to see the whole thing," Fiona instructed. After Brigid made a circle, Fiona nodded approvingly. "It does look really good on you," Fiona said. "I hate to say it, but I did a darn good job," she chuckled.

Brigid felt a little awkward as she stood before them, but she had to admit that the clothes did make her feel a little better. A knock on the front door caused them all to turn around and look towards it. "I bet that's her," Fiona said as she stood. "I told her she could close up a little early today."

"Oh, the psychic lady?" Holly asked.

Brigid shifted uncomfortably. She wasn't sure if she was ready to meet this woman. Yet a small voice in the back of her mind seemed to encourage it, as if it was saying, "What are you so afraid of? You know and trust Melanie and this woman was taught by her. Relax. After all, there can be more than one psychic in the world."

Brigid took a deep breath and tried to do as the voice instructed, but it wasn't as easy as she'd hoped. For some reason, the thought that this woman knew about her one moment in life that she truly wished she could hide really unsettled her.

Fiona opened the front door and happily greeted the woman. They smiled and hugged each other as if they were good friends who had spent years getting to know each other. Brigid walked over to Holly and sat down beside her on the couch.

"Is it weird that I feel excited to meet her?" Holly whispered.

Brigid shrugged, because in all honesty, she didn't share the same sentiment. The woman stepped inside. Brigid noticed her medium length layered hair and her bright, expressive green eyes. A smile spread across her full lips when she saw Brigid and Holly.

"Hello," she said softly with a small wave.

"Brigid, Holly, this is Abra. Abra, this is my sister Brigid and her daughter Holly," Fiona explained as she gestured towards them.

"Nice to meet you," Abra said with a smile. "I've heard a lot about both of you."

"Same," Holly said eagerly. "I'm glad we finally get to meet."

She turned back to Fiona. "I just stopped by to let you know that I closed everything up. I cleaned everything, top to bottom, and did a little straightening up in the back room as well," she said. "Here are the keys. Nobody had been in for quite a while, so I think you were right when you told me to close early today."

"Thank you," Fiona said. "I promise to get a key made for you. I just haven't had a chance to get over to the hardware store and actually do it," she sighed. "Please, come in and join us."

"I don't want to intrude," Abra said. Brigid noticed that Abra would look over at Holly and her and then quickly look away. It made her wonder if there was something wrong or if the woman was just nervous about meeting new people.

"No, not a bit," Fiona said as she turned. "Would you like something to drink?" She put her hand on Abra's shoulder and led her into the living room.

"No thanks, I'm good," Abra said as she slowly walked in the room and sat down in an armchair.

"Fiona says you're a psychic like Melanie," Holly blurted.

"Holly, really?" Brigid said as she turned toward Holly. "Maybe Abra doesn't want to talk about all of that."

"No, it's fine," Abra said with a nod. "I am, but I believe that Melanie and I have two different styles."

"Really?" Holly asked, intrigued. "I didn't realize there were different kinds of psychics."

"Oh, yes," Abra said. "I'm not quite as upfront as Melanie is. She seems to have no trouble telling people what she's sensing. I tend to hold back."

Brigid was a little surprised to hear that. "Why is that?" she found herself asking.

"I don't know. Maybe because I don't want people to think I'm weird or nosy or something like that. People often don't feel comfortable when you know things about them that they often think you shouldn't know," she shrugged.

There was something about Abra that made Brigid let some of her guard down, although she hadn't realized she'd even put it up. It was as if the woman had known what Brigid needed to hear. When Brigid thought about it, she realized she could sympathize with Abra.

What if she knew things about other people and they held that against her? Things that just came to her spontaneously? What if people thought she was evil, crazy, or whatever, just because of a few innocent hunches she'd gotten? Even so, for some reason, she still wasn't sure she could trust Abra.

"By the way, your blouse is really cute," Abra said to Brigid. "Where did you get it?"

"Fiona made it," Brigid said proudly as she touched the bow.

"That's amazing," Abra said excitedly as she turned toward Fiona. "Fiona, you have some serious talent. When are you going to start a clothing business?"

She and Fiona started talking, but Brigid couldn't concentrate on their conversation. She found herself looking inward and thinking about the past, about her parents, and her regrets.

Normally she pushed them so far down she almost forgot they existed, but now that they'd been brought up, it was as if they refused to stay hidden any longer. Being in the presence of a stranger who knew that about her seemed to be what had brought it up to the surface.

"Oh, you should get to know Missy," Holly said from beside her. The suddenness of her voice snapped Brigid back to reality.

"Who is Missy?" Abra asked curiously.

"She and her husband run the church," Brigid explained. She didn't want anyone to think she hadn't been paying attention, even though she'd seemingly checked out for a moment.

"I'm sure she'd love to hear your views," Holly said.

"I don't know," Abra said hesitantly. "Not everyone who is religious appreciates people like me."

"Missy is different," Fiona insisted. "She's as open-minded as they come. She'd probably agree with you on a lot of it. She loves to talk and debate about beliefs, but not in an aggressive way. She just really enjoys hearing about what other people believe."

"Well, in that case, I hope I'll get to meet her soon," Abra said as she cast a glance behind the couch where Brigid and Holly were sitting.

"I'm sorry, but do any of you know a female who was a rather young woman when she passed? Actually, she was probably around my age. She's got a mother energy about her, but she's far too young to be your mother, Brigid. Besides, I know what your mother feels like, and that's not who this is."

The suddenness of the change in conversation confused Brigid for a moment. She didn't realize what Abra had really said until she gave it a chance to sink in.

"It must be my mom," Holly said softly. Abra looked over at Brigid, but Holly shook her head. "My birth mom. Brigid adopted me after she died."

"I see," Abra said, nodding. There was no judgment or searching for more. She seemed to accept what Holly had just said and continued. "She's with you a lot. She's shorter than you are, and I see darker hair. I feel like it's hard for her to breathe."

She seemed to collect herself and shook off whatever she was feeling. "She's around and wants you to know that it really is her. There's some sort of situation that makes you wonder if it's her. I don't know what it is specifically, but she said you'd understand."

"I do," Holly said. "I see…"

"Please, don't tell me anything yet," Abra said as she held up one finger. "I don't want to seem rude, but it's easier for me if you don't. Not yet. I start to question myself if I have any sort of information. Sorry," she said, seemingly troubled that she'd interrupted Holly, but Holly just waved it away.

"She wants to thank you too," she continued as she turned towards Brigid. "She says she's so happy you stepped in to help and that you're doing a better job than she felt she could have done if she had lived. She gives me the feeling that you two are a team. It's as if she gives nudges from the other side, and then you take care of the real world things."

Brigid gave a soft smile. "I try to respect her memory."

"She said you're doing a great job. I feel a regret about family, but I'm getting a sense it's lifting. Does that make any sense?" she continued.

"Yes, it does," Holly nodded.

"It's like you've done something that she wished she could have done when she was alive. She wants me to express to you she's not upset. On the contrary, she's delighted." Abra stared at a spot on the floor as she spoke as if she was lost in thought.
"Oh, good," Holly sighed.

She looked at Holly and said, "You also found a piece of jewelry that was hers. She'd intended for you to have it, but she'd planned to give it to you later. She was the one guiding you to find it." Abra seemed to concentrate even harder. "And one other thing, she just wants you to know she's proud of you. Plain and simple. That's all she really has to say right now."

"That was amazing," Holly said with a tear in her eye.

Brigid had to agree. Part of her wished that Abra would tell her

34

about her parents, but another part, a bigger one, didn't want her to. She wasn't sure if she could handle it, and she was afraid she'd break down crying, which was something she didn't want to do in front of a stranger.

As the conversation continued, Brigid wondered if she'd ever feel at peace when she thought about her parents. She really wanted to, but she wasn't sure if it was possible. The guilt she felt was too heavy and restrictive. Instead, she did what she'd always done, she pushed it to the back of her mind and moved on.

CHAPTER SIX

Gage Morton simply did not like Holly Lewis. He wasn't sure what it was, but there was something about her that just irritated him. Maybe it was because she was such a know-it-all. She was never caught off guard by the teachers, and she always knew the answer when they called on her. She threw off the grading curve in every class. Holly was always there, with her homework done and a smile on her face. It nauseated him.

Sometimes he wished she'd get sick or something, so that everyone else didn't look so bad. He knew that probably wasn't the best thing to wish on a person, but he couldn't help it. If she could strategically get sick on a few days when pop quizzes were given, it sure would help his grades. Most of the teachers graded on a curve if it seemed like the class wasn't getting a concept, which really helped the people like him. Problem was, the curve always remained high because good old Holly's grade never failed to mess it up for everyone.

As he walked through the high school halls on his way to his locker, Gage waved to a few friends of his. Most of them were fellow football players. He didn't have much to do with anyone who wasn't on the team. He'd talk to some of the other smart kids when he needed some help with homework or something, but that was purely out of necessity.

He looked forward to his next class, since it was a computer class. It was called Computer Tech 4, but it really wasn't all that technical. They usually just did some sort of digital project while the teacher read a book. Because the class was so simple, he didn't have to take much of anything to class, so he usually just dropped everything off at his locker on his way to class.

"Hey, how was the history test?" he asked the girl a few lockers down from him. He could never remember her name, but he knew she had history in the morning. Her black hair was pulled into pigtails that fell forward on her shoulders. She turned, surprised to have someone talking to her.

"Not too bad. He covered most of it yesterday, so if you were paying attention and taking notes, you should be good," she said brightly. "I think most people did fairly well. Just depends on how much you listened." Shrugging, she closed her locker and walked away.

Gage nodded and turned towards his locker. Yesterday in history class he'd been too busy doodling in his notebook to pay attention. He just hadn't felt like dealing with school yesterday, and he'd been busy thinking about football practice. He'd mentally been running through the plays the team was going to practice after school.

There was only so much room in his brain for stuff. How was he supposed to remember football stuff and school stuff too? If the teacher was testing them on what they'd learned yesterday in class, Gage was definitely not going to do well. That is, unless he decided to test Gage on his plays. Because he executed those flawlessly yesterday. He considered skipping history, since it was his last class of the day after this one. He could always use the excuse that he'd had a doctor's appointment.

Gage shut the door to his locker, deciding he wouldn't worry about it right now. He normally didn't mind the computer class, so at least there was that to look forward to. It was a very slow and easy class, a time for his mind to not feel like it was being pulled in twenty different directions trying to remember everything.

He was one of those people who was just naturally good with computers. For now at least, he could focus on a class he wasn't failing, one where he could sit back and feel like he had it together. He'd worry about history when it was time for history.

As he made his way to class, he wondered what the next project would be. They'd wrapped up their last one and today was the day his teacher would tell them what they'd be working on next. He'd heard from someone they were going to be building a website, which he thought would be very interesting.

He'd played around with doing that many times when he was bored at home. Something like that should be a piece of cake for him. How great would it be if, for once, he was at the top of the class because he already knew how to do something?

Gage walked into his computer class and sat down at his station. The computers were lined up against the walls with dividers between each one. He guessed they were there to prevent people from cheating, but who needed to cheat in computers?

He liked the computer classes because they were so much easier for him than some of the others, like math. He needed at least one easy class to help his GPA. The bell rang, and he ran his hand through his red hair. The countdown was on until history class.

"Okay, class," Mr. Pelham, the teacher, said as he entered the room. "I've been debating about what to do for our next project. We've been learning a lot about how websites are built and the various components that go into them. I heard about something one of my students in a lower level class did, and I thought it would be the perfect teaching opportunity."

Great, Gage thought. *Here we go again. Someone's making things harder on the rest of us.*

"Holly Lewis has built a website for a new B & B in town, and I think we should all take a look at it and see if we can figure out how she did it," the teacher began as he shut the lights off and switched on the flat screen TV that was connected to his computer.

Gage looked around as the teacher droned on and on about how great the website was, but he couldn't bring himself to listen. Even if he'd wanted to, he wouldn't have been able to. Just the fact that it was something Holly had done made him want to punch a wall. Who the heck was she to do this and make everyone else look bad?

He looked around, hoping that other students felt the same way he did, but everyone else in class was staring intently at the screen. It was as if they were all under her spell, too. Was he the only one who saw how irritating she was? How she was making things harder for everyone?

Fine, he thought as he looked around. *You can all fall in line and worship Holly all you want, but not me. I'm not going to allow her to set the pace for me. I'm my own person and that's that.*

Didn't everyone else see that the teachers put her up on a pedestal like she was some sort of wonder child? Sure, she was smart, but so what? There were plenty of other smart kids around, and no one talked about them all the time. Why was it that this girl and the amazing things she managed to do were constantly being pushed in his face?

Gage pulled out his notebook and started to doodle. At this point he was willing to do anything if it meant not listening to someone talk about Holly. If he'd been told doing one hundred pushups would make the teacher stop talking about her, he willingly would have done them. Even though just one look at his plump body would let anyone know that there was no way he could complete them. After all, he was a lineman, not a quarterback. His team needed him to be big.

"My challenge for all of you is to build your own website," Mr. Pelham said. "We have a local server they can run on, so it will appear just as it would if it was live. You can make the website for anything, such as a local business, the school, anything you think you can improve upon. And hey, you never know. Someone may like your site and want to buy it. Today I want you to search for ideas. Try to think creatively and outside the box. You know I grade for effort, so show me you put some real thought into your efforts."

As everyone hurried to get to work on their websites, all Gage could think about was how Holly had done it again. She'd created something for everyone to see just how smart she was. Now there was a testament to her genius online for the whole world to see.

Whoop dee doo. Wasn't that just fabulous? Gage thought. *If only there was a way to get rid of it. To completely just take her website down and be like, "Hmm, maybe she's not as awesome as you all think she is, huh?" Or if it was buggy and crashed all the time, that would be great. Then maybe everyone would see that Holly wasn't all that awesome after all.*

A small part of Gage told him that it wasn't like the project was all her fault. The teacher still would have them doing something, but the fact that he used her website as an excuse just made Gage not want to do it at all. If it had been anyone else, he would have been willing to go along with the whole thing. But the fact it was Holly Lewis made his brain completely check out. When her name was mentioned he was getting to the point where he just tuned out and went somewhere else.

Once Mr. Pelham sat down at his desk and went back to reading his book, Gage began to think more and more about getting rid of Holly's website. The thought consumed him. All he wanted to do was wreck the entire thing. He knew she hadn't built it for herself, but that didn't matter. Whoever it was probably held her on a pedestal too. He couldn't stand the thought of it being out there in the internet, drawing attention to itself. If only you could blow up a website....

But wait, couldn't he? They'd learned about the drag and drop style website builders out there. Seeing all the effects on the site, that was the only explanation. There was no way she was able to learn to code that well and that fast. She must have used something, and if she had, he should be able to figure it out.

Rather than researching the project Mr. Pelham had given them as their next assignment, Gage went on a hunt to figure out exactly how Holly had managed to build the site. If he knew how she built it, he knew he could figure out how to take it down. He wasn't quite sure how, but he'd figure it out. She wasn't the only one around here with a brain.

CHAPTER SEVEN

Brigid was sitting at her desk, editing one of her client's recent novels when her phone buzzed letting her know that she had a text message. Picking up her phone, she was happy to see it was a message from Missy.

Hey, I haven't been able to come by and see the new B & B, it said. *I was wondering if maybe you were free and I could drive over there now?*

Brigid smiled. It had been a while since she'd been able to spend time with her friend. Life had just become so busy for each of them that they hadn't had a chance to catch up.

Sure, come on by. I'm the only one at home right now, so I can show you around, she texted back and then stood up from her desk. She needed a break anyway, so an unexpected visit from Missy was a welcome relief. Sitting in front of her computer for long periods of time always ended up straining her eyes. Having a short break would probably be helpful. No need to overdo it today.

Brigid walked out of her office and picked up the great room a little. She knew Missy wouldn't mind if it looked a little cluttered, but it was more of a personal thing with Brigid. There was no need to have dishes and Holly's dirty clothes laying around. A few minutes later there was a knock at the door.

"Hello!" they both cried out as Brigid opened the door and they hugged. "It seems like it's been forever," Missy said.

"I agree," Brigid sighed as she let her friend in. "I think it's been a month or more."

"I know, I've been planning on stopping by for what feels like a month now, but time always seems to get away from me," Missy huffed. "So today I told myself I wouldn't let another day go by without reaching out to you."

"I'm so glad you did," Brigid said with a smile. "So, are you ready to go see our almost ready for the grand opening B & B?"

She led Missy out the front door and they followed the brick pathway that connected the two houses.

"Your little path is so cute. I love it," Missy cooed.

"Thanks," Brigid said. "The grass was starting to get thin from us walking back and forth so much, so we laid the bricks and let them sink in a bit. I think it gives the B & B a more natural feel."

"For sure," Missy agreed. "And it looks like it's been here for years."

They made their way to the front door and Brigid unlocked it. "Welcome to the New Dawn Bed & Breakfast," she said as she pushed the door open. She watched Missy's face as it went from mildly curious to awe. It was as if she'd had certain expectations and they'd just been blown out of the water.

"Brigid, this is gorgeous!" Missy said as she stepped inside. She tried to look at everything all at once, turning her head one way and then the other. "It's so comfortable and cozy."

The living room area was set up similar to a waiting room, but in a much more comfortable way. There was a long wooden table which served as the registration area. Linc had debated on building a check-in counter, but they'd finally decided against it, feeling it would be too much like a hotel rather than a B & B.

The two-story wall of glass in the dining room seemed to transport the nearby forest into the house. Plants were strategically tucked in various places, keeping a natural and cozy feeling to go along with the darker colors of the walls and the wood. "Brigid, it really feels like a high-end B & B. Not saying I expected it to be cheap or anything…"

"No, I completely understand," Brigid said as she held up her hand. She knew exactly what her friend was trying to say. She'd had the same feeling when she saw it all put together. "It turned out far better than I was expecting."

She led her friend into the dining room and pointed out what had been hers, what had been Linc's, and the furniture they'd had to buy. "Most of the things in this room were his," she explained. "When he lived here, he set up the dining room the way he'd always wanted one to look, with plenty of wooden beams, a high ceiling, and floor-to-ceiling windows. We decided to leave it that way."

"I'm sure your guests will love it," Missy gushed. "It almost has a log cabin feeling without actually being one. Not that there's anything wrong with log cabins, but you know what I mean."

When they were in the hall, Brigid pointed out the family picture they'd hung. "This is the same one that's on our website," Brigid explained. "Holly's friend Levi took it and we loved it so much we had a print made. We wanted something that represented us as a whole."

"Aww," Missy said as she gently touched it. "I can't help but feel a little emotional," Missy said as a tear escaped from the corner of her eye. "To think I've watched your family come together. I still remember that first night at the bookstore when you and Linc had just recently met."

"I know," Brigid said, feeling a little sentimental herself. She put her arm around Missy, and they both stared at the picture for a moment longer. "I was so close to not even going. I just didn't feel like visiting with a bunch of people, you know.

"But I met Linc and the next thing I knew, I'd invited him to the party. It seems like it wasn't long after that when Holly came into my life. It was as if we were all drawn together, kind of like magnets." She lightly touched the picture with her fingers before both women ended up wiping their eyes and continuing on.

"Next I'll show you the room Holly decorated."

"She told me she was going to get to do one," Missy said, intrigued. "I was curious as to how she'd do it, because she has such unique taste. She's very feminine but not girly, if that makes any sense."

"I know exactly what you mean, and I really like the way she did her room," Brigid said as they stood outside the door. Next to it was a plaque that dubbed it "Holly's Room." "You're right, Missy. She made it feminine, but not so much that a man would be uncomfortable in it. I think she struck just the right balance."

The first thing Missy noticed when the door was opened were the deep purple walls. "Oh wow," she said as she stepped inside. The rustic wooden floor had an area rug in grey tones. The curtains were a soft grey that almost glowed with the light. The duvet was somewhat Moroccan looking with its details. In purple and grey, it united the room.

"I would have never thought of this combination, but it's beautiful," Missy said as she continued to look at the rest of the details throughout the room.

"I know, Holly put a lot of thought into this one," Brigid said.

Missy paused at the painting above the short dresser. It was a landscape with a sunset that had various shades of the colors that were in the room.

"She did a great job," Missy finally said as she turned and walked back towards the door.

"Quite frankly, I think Holly's room turned out to be the best out of all of them. And surprisingly enough, she spent the least amount of money," Brigid said with a touch of pride in her voice.

"Good girl," Missy said as they stepped out into the hall, "She must be a great bargain hunter."

"She needs to teach me her tricks," Brigid said, "because I think I'm the one who spent the most."

"Nothing wrong with having expensive taste," Missy said simply.

"There is if you can't afford to live expensively," Brigid laughed. "Here's my room. Linc did the last two."

"Really?" Missy said surprised.

Brigid nodded as she opened the door to the next room. The duvet was a floral print with a dark green background and the walls were a simple white. The furniture was all dark wood and the bed was a beautiful four poster.

"This seems like a room that would be great to relax in," Missy said as she touched a rocking chair tucked in the corner.

"Thanks, I thought so, too," Brigid said with a smile. "That's what our goal is for our guests. We're trying to create a place they can relax."

"Well, you've definitely achieved that," Missy said.

They continued on to the next room which was done in a blue theme. With darker wood, it was a bit more masculine than some of the other rooms, looking more like a study than a bedroom. Linc had even put a few books in this one, just in case the guests needed something to read. Brigid was still debating if she wanted to do something similar in the other rooms.

She didn't want to bring it up to Linc, though. She was afraid he'd overthink the whole thing and have them swapping books throughout the rooms, looking for his favorite combinations. As if any of the guests would really care about which books were in each room.

Missy was commenting on how lovely everything was when her phone began to ring. "I'm sorry," she said as she pulled it out of her pocket. "I swear, some days this thing just never stops ringing."

She gave Brigid an apologetic smile as she answered it. Brigid knew how busy Missy was. There were always people wanting to volunteer, donate, or were looking for help themselves, and Missy was the one who coordinated it all. Fundraisers, family nights, and everything else that involved the community. Residents of Cottonwood Springs had come to rely on her to get the job done.

Yes, she was very busy trying to oversee everything. After a brief conversation she hung up and sighed. "I swear, that man would not make it without me," she said as she shook her head.

"Say no more," Brigid laughed. "I think I understand already."

"I have to run, but if I don't get to see you before your grand opening, I wish you luck," she said as they walked towards the front door.

"Thank you so much," Brigid said. "It means a lot to me."

"You're going to do great," Missy said. "Just you wait and see." They said their good byes and Brigid waved as Missy headed to her car. Before she locked up the B & B, Brigid decided that now was as good a time as any to add those books to the rooms. Linc was at the grocery store, so he wouldn't be around to ask a million questions and wonder about the personalities of their potential guests.

She walked over to their house and headed for her office, which was where she kept most of her books. She didn't want to put her absolute favorites in the B & B in case they ended up disappearing with a guest, but she didn't want to put boring ones in there, either.

Eventually she settled on a couple of time travel romances, some non-fiction self-help books, and a few biographies she'd found fascinating. Looking at her choices, she decided she pretty much had something for everyone. She put them in a couple of plastic bags to make them easier to carry and headed back to the B & B.

While she was walking across the yard, she started to mentally place the books in certain rooms. As she did, she realized with a chuckle that she was doing the same thing Linc often did, imagining a certain type of guest in each of the different rooms.

She shook her head, wondering if Linc was starting to rub off on her. Then she decided it was probably just his excitement that was rubbing off. And who couldn't be excited with him working them up to the big day as if it was Christmas? Of course, that was part of the reason she loved him so much. He was like a big puppy dog, excited and ready for anything.

Once she'd put the books in each room and closed the doors, she went back to the house. Jett met her at the door, happy to see her. "Nice to see you too, lazy bones," she said with a smile as she reached down to pet him. He seemed to smile at her before she turned towards the couch and sat down. Jett followed close behind, glad to be in her company.

"Maybe you're like a lucky penny, Jett. Things have all been great ever since you came into my life. Is that it? Are you like a genie granting me wishes?"

Jett panted in response and Brigid smiled. She looked at the ceiling above, thinking about what Abra had said at Fiona's house. Is it possible that Holly's mom and her parents were looking out for them? She'd like to think so. It wasn't like things were bad in her life, in fact it was the complete opposite.

But still, she liked the thought of having heavenly helpers guiding her along once in a while. It was nice to know she didn't have to do everything on her own, and that if she needed to talk, there were people on the other side who would be more than willing to listen to her.

"Thank you," she said to the air. "Thank you for everything."

CHAPTER EIGHT

Rich Jennings was at the grocery store, picking up a few things he needed for the grilled chicken he was planning to make for dinner. He was also thinking about what he'd make for breakfast the next morning for his guests at his B & B. As he turned toward the produce section, he saw Milly. Milly was one of the town gossips and he'd been dealing with her ever since he'd been the sheriff of Cottonwood Springs.

After Rich's sister had been murdered, the family B & B needed someone to take it over. By then, he'd had enough of law enforcement work, so he resigned as sheriff and found his happiness serving others in a slightly different way, as the owner-operator of a B & B.

"Good afternoon, Sh- I mean, Mr. Jennings," she said as she batted her eyelashes at him. Milly was an older woman who could be anywhere from her early seventies to late eighties. She just had that ageless look about her. She'd been alone for far too long and took it upon herself to flirt with Rich every chance she got. She always did have trouble remembering that he wasn't the sheriff anymore.

"Good afternoon, Milly. I've told you time and time again to please call me Rich," he said politely. He knew she was just trying to be friendly, but sometimes he did get a little tired of putting on a show for her.

She giggled slightly and nodded her head. "Oh, that's right. It must have slipped my mind. How's your B & B going?" she asked as she stepped closer to him.

"Actually, quite well," he said proudly. "Just picking up a few things to feed my guests and me. It's nice having people staying there. I'd much rather be cooking for guests than not."

"I couldn't believe it when I heard that new guy was going to open a B & B in Cottonwood Springs. What's with these city folks thinking they can just come in here and take over?" she asked grumpily.

At first, Rich was confused. He didn't know of anyone that was new in town, but then he recalled how anyone who wasn't born in Cottonwood Springs was a new person to Milly. "I think it's wonderful," Rich said. "I often get overbooked, so it will be nice for me to have somewhere to refer them," he said.

He didn't want to stand there and explain how he'd actually been the one to plant the seed in Linc's mind to convert his empty house into a B & B. It was best to not give Milly any more information than she already knew. Plenty of people had learned that the hard way.

"You're a much better person than I am, that's all I'm going to say about it," she said as she stuck her nose in the air. Her look told him that she wanted to say more, even if her words said otherwise.

"And why do you say that?" he asked as he turned toward the tomatoes looking for ripe ones. He wasn't sure how this woman had come to the conclusion that Linc's B & B could be bad for Rich.

"Well, think about it," she said in a hushed tone. "What if they start stealing your business?" She was acting as though there may be people listening in to their conversation, but no one else was even in this part of the store at the moment.

"I don't think Linc and Brigid would do that," he said as he shook his head. "They aren't that kind of people." He had to hold back a chuckle at the thought. He knew them both far too well to ever believe they'd do something intentionally to hurt his business. It just wasn't in their nature.

"But that doesn't mean if you refer someone over to them, the person won't decide they like their B & B better. After all, it is newer. These fancy city people who come to Cottonwood Springs for a little get away tend to think newer is better. That's why they tear down anything old with history and replace it with something new. It's like those darn coffeeshops you see everywhere." She tsked and shook her head. "Why, if I was a building, they would have torn me down years ago."

"I don't know about that, Milly. Old beauties still stick around," he said with a wink. He thought if he gave her a little attention, maybe she'd wrap up the conversation so he could be on his way. He'd heard enough from Milly about this situation for now. He wanted to finish his shopping and head home.

"Oh, you flatterer, you," she said playfully. "I'm just saying. If you don't watch out, you may find yourself without any guests and then where will you be? I'd hate to see something that's been in your family for so long disappear like a puff of smoke. Especially to someone who's not from around here." She shook her head and pushed her cart along toward the cucumbers and resumed shopping. "You have a good day now," she said as she moved along.

Rich shook his head. He wasn't sure why Milly would think something like that. After all, Linc and Brigid were good people. Yet as he continued shopping in the produce section, something about the conversation began to nag at him.

What if there is some truth to what she said? He started to wonder. *What if after I refer someone over to Linc, they never come back to my B & B? Will I be put out of business?*

Rich began to worry. He didn't know why he hadn't seen a flaw in his plan before. Would he end up going out of business because he'd urged them to open a B & B? He shook his head. He couldn't allow himself to begin thinking that way. Besides, it was a little late for that now.

Linc and Brigid had put so much time and effort into building their B & B, it wasn't as if he could change his mind and tell them to stop. They were literally weeks away from their grand opening. If he remembered right, they should be getting ready to take reservations on their website any time now.

Just thinking about their website made him even more nervous. For the first time he realized he didn't have nearly the online presence that they did. He was still pretty much using the same system his sister had used before her death, and that had been several years ago.

Of course, he'd advertised in a few places, but that was about all he'd done that was new. What if somehow Linc's B & B became number one and his dropped to second? Would that disrupt his business enough that it would be in trouble?

Leaving the produce section, Rich did his best to forget about it. He could always go over his online presence later, but for now things seemed to be working okay. Surely if something was wrong with his plan, he would have seen it by now. But a seed of doubt had been planted in his mind, and no matter how hard he tried to push the entire thing from his mind, it still lingered.

Finishing up his shopping, he distractedly went through the check-out line. He picked up a new crossword puzzle book for later as he stood there, waiting for the girl behind the counter to ring up his things. She told him his total and after swiping his credit card, he headed out to his car.

Well, surely if they end up getting booked solid, Brigid and Linc would send people over to me, he rationalized as he drove home. When he tried to imagine a situation where Brigid or Linc was anything but helpful, it didn't feel right. But the thought still remained that maybe they wouldn't have to do anything. After all, if their B & B was better than his, the bottom line was that people just wouldn't come to his. It wouldn't matter how many people they referred to him if the referrals weren't interested in his B & B.

Wasn't that how the big box stores like Walmart had often taken out the old hometown mom and pop stores? Those bigger, fancier places had something that the little stores just couldn't compete with. Then the income of those stores got tighter, which forced them to further restrict their inventory. It was simply a vicious chain of events that left the little store owner decimated.

But Brigid and Linc weren't some big corporation, he reminded himself. They were friends and neighbors. That was what he had running through his mind as he pulled into the parking area beside his B & B. He got his grocery bags out of his SUV and entered through the side entrance that led into the kitchen.

Rich unpacked his groceries but he still couldn't get the conversation with Milly out of his mind. Unfortunately, that little seed had begun to sprout. He needed the B & B to keep the memory of his sister and parents alive. He hoped to someday have someone to share it with, but he had to keep it going for that to happen. If he didn't, what would he have to offer his future wife? After putting away the groceries, he decided to see what Brigid and Linc had done online to attract guests.

He sat down at his computer and started searching the New Dawn B & B online to see what he could find out about it. He wanted to know what someone might see if they looked for Brigid and Linc's B & B. Soon, he was finding social media profiles, fancy websites, and ads. He revised his search to include just bed and breakfasts in the Cottonwood Springs area, to see how theirs showed up compared to his.

When the results came up, he saw that their B & B was right below his. Whoever had helped them with their website design had certainly done their research. Getting his results to show up had taken months of research for Rich. Of course, he'd had to learn all about keywords and things like that, but it had still taken up a lot of his free time. He wondered just how much Holly might have helped them with their website and advertising. He'd heard she made the website, but had she helped with the advertising too? If so, maybe he should hire her.

Rich began to think that he needed a way to slow them down. Maybe if they didn't have a strong start, everything would be okay. If they were forced to pace themselves, maybe the two B & B's could work together. But he had a sinking feeling that if they took off running, it could be the beginning of the end for him. He needed to come up with a way to make them look not quite so put together. His time as sheriff had given him a lot of contacts. Maybe someone could help him figure out a way to make that beautiful website of theirs less attractive...

CHAPTER NINE

"I can't believe it's already time for spring break," Holly sighed as she sat down at the dinner table. "Like, where did the first part of the school year go, anyway? I swear it was just last month we were doing Christmas. Then the next day it was Valentine's Day. It's as if everything is just jumping forward at warp speed." She seemed almost frustrated by the idea that time had flown by so fast.

"I agree," Brigid said as she pulled plates from the kitchen cabinet and placed them on the counter. "Before long we're going to be welcoming our first visitors. It seems like only yesterday Linc was over at the B & B driving the construction crew crazy."

"I wasn't driving them crazy, per se. It was more like I was encouraging them to work as efficiently as possible," Linc said with a chuckle as he began plating the dinner meal. "I didn't want to deal with any more delays than were absolutely necessary. I'm just glad Fiona and Brandon agreed that if we ever want to take a trip, they'd manage the B & B for us. I didn't want to have to totally close up if it wasn't necessary."

"I have to admit that I was a little surprised she volunteered," Brigid said. "But Fiona was right. Between her running the bookstore and Brandon being the manager of the ski resort, they'd be the ones with the most experience. Plus, we know we can definitely trust them with everything."

"Fiona could probably do it with her eyes closed," Holly scoffed. "That lady is definitely a business woman. I don't blame you for having her as a backup. Who else could run your business for you that would be any better than her?"

"Nobody," Brigid agreed as she carried their plates to the table. "You know, Holly, when I talked to her on the phone, she mentioned something about having you make a website for her for both the clothes she makes and the bookstore. She wants Levi to do the photography too."

"That's cool," Holly nodded. "Sure, I can if she'd like me to. My classes this year are fairly easy, so I don't really have the homework I had to deal with last year. Actually, it's kind of nice." Her phone vibrated and she picked it up to see who it was. "Hey, do we have enough food for Wade? He just sent me a message and wanted to know if it's okay if he comes by." She looked from Brigid to Linc, unsure of which of them would be answering.

"Sure," Linc said. "Tell him to come on over and that we'll have a plate waiting for him." He pulled another plate out and filled it before carrying it and his to the table and sitting down. "There's always room at our table for Wade. He's a good kid."

"He really likes your cooking," Holly said as she started to dig in. "The one thing that bummed him out about working was that he was going to miss your cooking." She smiled and said, "He's going to be so excited he'll probably eat way too much like last time."

"We can always send him home with some leftovers," Linc winked. "After all, I made enough to feed an army." In a few minutes, they heard a knock on the door and Wade opened it.

"Hey guys," he said with a little wave before shutting the door behind him. "Sorry to interrupt." He looked sheepish as he turned around and faced them.

"No, please. Come on in," Brigid insisted. "There's a plate for you next to Holly. We don't mind having you join us one bit. You know you're always welcome here. We completely understand how tough it can be to find the time to get away from work these days."

"Thank you," he said as he joined them. "It smells great and I'm starving."

"Well, in that case, dig in," Linc said happily.

The conversation started by Wade talking about how the ski lodge was going. He told them all about what a usual day was like for him there. After that, they all took turns talking about their day and what they'd been doing.

"When will you start taking reservations for the B & B?" Wade asked.

"Next week," Linc said with a nod. "I have to tell you that I'll probably be on pins and needles until the first reservation comes in."

"Why's that?" Wade asked. "It's sure to be a hit."

"I wish I was as confident as you are," Linc sighed.

"You don't think it's going to go well?" Holly asked, surprised.

"I don't know," Linc admitted. "Honestly, I think it's just nerves. I mean, logically I know everything's in place. But there's just this little buzz in the back of my head that keeps making me doubt myself."

"I had that same feeling when I branched out and started editing on my own," Brigid said. "I was sure none of my clients would follow me, and I'd be sunk before I even started. I think it's natural to worry like that."

"Really?" Wade asked. "That kind of surprises me."

"Why?" Brigid asked. "You think I'm just confident in everything?"

"Well, kind of," Wade admitted. "I mean, you're so calm and collected all the time."

"I don't feel that way," she said as she shook her head. "Most of the time I'm just winging it."

"Well, then you wing it really well," Wade laughed.

"So why didn't you want to eat dinner at home?" Holly asked Wade. "Not that I mind you being here, but I'm just curious."

"Remember my dad's friend who had been hanging out with Zeus before he went missing?" Wade asked after taking a big bite. "He's started coming over to drink beer and watch some football games on TV with Dad."

"You don't like him?" Holly asked.

"It's not that," Wade said shaking his head. "He's a great guy, but boy does he eat. I barely get anything to eat when he comes over."

"Well, maybe he likes your mom's cooking," Brigid pointed out.

"I know he does," Wade nodded. "He's said so. I'm beginning to think he doesn't cook, so he really likes a home-cooked meal. Besides, I don't mind. Anyway, I'd rather eat over here." He grinned really wide, making everyone else smile.

"That's really sweet of you, Wade," Brigid said. "And you know you're always welcome here."

"Thanks, I really appreciate it," he said. "May I have seconds?"

"You can get thirds, if you want," Linc said. "I made plenty. These ladies don't eat nearly enough. I keep trying to plump them up, but it isn't working," he said, sounding defeated.

Holly and Brigid laughed. "You're not plumping me up, mister," Brigid said playfully. "If I get any plumper, people are going to start thinking I'm eating for two."

"Would that be terrible?" Linc asked.

"It is if I'm not!" Brigid said exasperated.

"Well, you're not much fun," Linc said, pretending to pout.

Holly and Wade laughed at the interaction and Brigid just shook her head. "Sometimes I don't know what to do with you," she sighed.

"Sure you do," Linc said with a grin. "Just love me and let me do my thing. Everything else moves along like clockwork."

"Is that so?" she said with a raised brow as he leaned closer to give her a kiss on the cheek.

"It is," he said as he kissed her. "You know it's true."

Jett pushed in between the two of them, as if he felt he should be a part of the embrace too.

"Oh, Jett," Brigid chuckled. "We can't possibly forget about you, can we? You're like another big, four-legged kid, aren't you?" She scratched behind his ears, in his favorite spot. She could tell by the leg that began to thump on the floor in a rhythmic manner that he enjoyed it.

"Jett is almost one of those dogs that you'd think would be impossible to forget he's there, since he's so big. But he really is quiet until he wants something," Wade pointed out. "He's the complete opposite of my dog, Zeus."

"Oh really?" Brigid asked. "Can Zeus be a pain?"

"Only when he knows you have something good," Wade chuckled.

"In a way, he's like Lucky," Holly pointed out. "Maybe that's why

TROUBLE AT THE NEW DAWN B & B

Zeus doesn't get along with him, because they're too much alike."

"That's very possible," Linc agreed. "People can be that way too. I once worked with a guy who absolutely hated this other man in the office. He complained about the guy's work ethic and how much the other man complained, but he never seemed to realize that he acted the exact same way! He spent so much time complaining and worrying about what everyone else was doing, he hardly ever got his work done on time."

"But I thought opposites were supposed to attract," Holly said thoughtfully.

"Maybe sometimes, but I think on occasion, opposites just explode," Linc joked. "

To change the subject, I made an apple pie today. Any takers?"

It was unanimous. Everyone wanted a piece of the pie and were amazed that Linc had made the filling with apples frozen from last fall. They decided it was easily the best apple pie they'd ever had.

CHAPTER TEN

After dinner, Holly and Wade went to her room to watch their favorite TV show together with Lucky hot on their heels. Linc and Brigid moved to the couch in the great room while Jett cleaned everyone's plates. Brigid had learned that using the dog as a way to pre-rinse their dishes helped the dishwasher work even better, plus it made Jett happy.

"I didn't realize you were so nervous about everything," Brigid said softly once she heard Holly's TV come on. She'd known that Linc had been a little anxious, but not to the extent that he'd admitted to at dinner.

"It's no big deal," Linc sighed. "I know it's probably all in my head. That's why I didn't say anything. You know how it can be when your mind is racing, and you just want to get something over with."

"Still, I want you to feel like you can tell me anything," Brigid said. "I don't want you to think that you can't come to me with something like that. It kind of hurt my feelings when I realized you'd been keeping it from me."

"I'm sorry," he said as he pulled her closer. "It wasn't intentional. I didn't want to bother you with something that I knew was no big deal. I mean, this thing will either work or it won't. No amount of worrying will make it go one way or the other. Only time will tell in the end if I just wasted a ton of time and money."

"I know," she sighed. "I just wish you'd realize how much I believe in you. I think with your love of cooking and people, not to mention the way you seem to draw people out, you'll be amazing at this. I wouldn't have stood behind it if I didn't feel that way. It won't be a waste of time and money, you'll see. You just have to have faith in yourself."

She smiled softly and touched his face. Her fingers then moved to his temples and traced the sprinkling of grey there. She loved Linc so much that sometimes it surprised her. Especially in moments like this when she got to see his soft and vulnerable side. Not that she didn't love the confident and expressive Linc, because she did. But this other side of him was very touching, and a part of him that that was rarely revealed.

"That really means a lot to me," Linc said as he kissed her cheek. "You know, maybe we should have another piece of that apple pie."

"Aren't you full?" Brigid laughed as she pulled away just enough to look him in the eye. Linc was always thinking about dessert.

"Well, I mean... I'm never too full for dessert or a second dessert," he began. "You know that."

"Where do you put it all?" she chuckled as she playfully smacked him with her hand. "It's a good thing you're so active or you'd weigh four hundred pounds by now."

"And what if I did?" he said with a smirk. "Would you still love me?"

"Of course I would," she said as she leaned closer and kissed him. She ran her fingers through his hair as she deepened the kiss.

"Hey guys," Holly said carefully from her door. "Did you do something to the website?"

Brigid and Linc pulled apart and looked at each other. "For the B & B?" Linc asked. "No, why?"

"Check it on your phones. Make sure it's not just me," she said, her voice wavering slightly with uncertainty. She came into the great room with Wade following her. She looked concerned, and that worried Brigid.

Tossing back the blanket that they'd draped across their laps, Brigid reached for her phone. Linc did the same. "What's wrong?" she asked as she found the browser and started typing the address. She could feel her pulse starting to quicken with worry. Holly wouldn't have sounded like that if everything was fine.

"It's just not coming up," Holly said. "I tried it a couple of times, but it won't do it. I'm not sure if my computer is just being dumb, though. I'm really hoping that's what it is. Really, really hoping."

"I can't get it to come up either," Linc said shaking his head and looking at Brigid.

"Me neither," Brigid said as she kept hitting refresh. Instead of the beautiful website, all she got was an error screen. It was as if the website had never existed. Brigid felt a sinking feeling overtaking her. How could this be happening?

"Something's not right," Holly said as she returned to her room. In a few moments she was back with her laptop. She set it down on the coffee table and pulled her hair back with a hair tie. She looked mad and determined all at once. Wade followed her and sat on the arm of the chair she was in, watching what she was doing.

"What are you going to do?" he asked.

"I'm going to try to log into the back end and see if I can find it that way," she explained. "Maybe the hosting company is just having an issue or maybe even the domain provider." Her forehead bunched in concentration as she stared at the screen. Her fingers started moving swiftly over the keys.

"Huh?" Brigid said as she blinked quickly. "Would someone please translate what you just said, so that us old folks can understand what's going on?"

"It's kind of like this," Wade began. "Think of your website as a house. The domain name is what people type to get there, so it's like the address for your house. The hosting is kind of like the land you build your house on. So with a website, if the hosting, or land, is having problems, you won't see your house. Same for the domain. If there is any sort of technical issue, all the pieces fall out of their place.

"I think Holly's hoping it's something like that. Maybe the hosting provider is doing some sort of maintenance, and it's just down for the time being."

"I see," Linc said as he leaned forward. "So how can you tell?"

"Damnit!" Holly cried out, surprising everyone. She looked a little shocked at herself and bashfully said, "Sorry." Her cheeks grew flushed. "I can't even get into the back end," she explained. "My login won't work."

"What does that mean?" Brigid asked. She was starting to wonder if something else was going on. How could a login suddenly not work? Was it too late to start learning more about computers so she could understand what the heck was going on?

"I'm not sure. It's almost like someone got into it and removed me from the site. But who could do that and why?" Holly asked as she looked up. "I mean, it's just a B & B. What would be the point in taking our website down? It doesn't make any sense at all."

"I don't like this," Brigid said quickly. "It doesn't feel right." She stood up from the couch and began to pace. Her gut was telling her that this wasn't a random thing. "How can we find out how this happened?"

"I'm online with tech support now to make sure it's not something on their end," Holly said as she focused on her screen.

"I'll be able to tell you for sure if it's them or someone messing with us in just a moment."

"But why would someone want to mess up the website?" Wade asked. "I mean, you guys aren't even taking reservations yet. It was essentially just a bunch of pictures."

"Why do people do any of the things they do?" Brigid asked as she continued to pace back and forth. She wanted to convince herself that it was a technical glitch and that any moment Holly would tell her they were back online and everything was okay. But she knew better. Deep down, she had that feeling of dread when you know something is just not right.

"People do bad things all the time for the simplest of reasons. Look at all the cases I've worked on. Even something like jealousy can trigger someone to do very bad things." She turned to Linc. "Did you upset anyone lately?"

"Me?" he asked, genuinely shocked. "I don't think so."

"Hmm," she said as she continued to think. She didn't feel it was a coincidence. Someone had managed to get into the website and take it down. But who? And what would be their motive for doing something so damaging?

She didn't have a clue how hard it would be to do something like that. Would it only take a few clicks? If it did, and the person knew what they were doing, it wouldn't take much. And from how easily Holly put the thing together, she wondered if some young person had done it as if it was some kind of a game.

"Someone hacked us," Holly said as she leaned back with a huff. "Everything else is fully operational. It's like the website was just taken down. My login page is there, but it keeps saying it doesn't recognize me."

"Can you get the company to let you in?" Linc asked hopefully.

"Nope," she said as she shook her head. "They don't handle that stuff. This is on me. I should have safeguarded it better. I just didn't think it was that big of a deal yet. I should have known better," she repeated as she sighed. "If I'd put more security in there, this wouldn't have happened." Frustrated, she slammed down the lid to her laptop.

"No, Holly, this isn't your fault." Brigid said as she stopped pacing. Wade was rubbing Holly's shoulders, trying to make her feel better. "You had absolutely no reason to think someone would do something like this. Nor would I. I'm going to give the sheriff a call and see what he knows about this sort of thing. Maybe he or someone he knows can help us out."

Holly nodded. "Okay. I'm going to see if I can find anything else out myself," she said as she picked up her laptop and headed back to her room. Wade, looking worried, followed her.

As Brigid picked up her phone, she noticed Linc sitting completely still. "Hey, are you okay?" she asked.

He looked up at her and his eyes were filled with uncertainty. "Why would someone do this?"

"I don't know," she responded as she sat down beside him and took his hand in hers. "But we're going to find out. That I promise you."

"Do you really think I could have made someone mad and they did this to get back at me?" he asked.

Brigid paused. She should have thought about her words earlier. Linc had already been so unsure of himself and then this happened. Accusing him of making someone mad wasn't going to help anything.

"No," she said shaking her head. "I didn't mean it like that. It's just, you know how people are. They can get upset at the smallest things. I thought maybe someone had possibly gotten upset with you for some dumb reason. After all, this B & B is your baby, your pet project. If someone wanted to hurt you, this would be how they could do it."

"No, it's not my baby," Linc said standing. "You are. Holly is. This B & B is just a business. A way for us to make money, be together, and enjoy ourselves. You and Holly are what matter to me."

"I appreciate that," Brigid said with a smile. "You're the most important thing to me, too." She stepped closer to him and touched his arm. "Which is why I won't be able to rest until I know who did this. As far as I'm concerned, they're going down."

CHAPTER ELEVEN

"Thank you for coming over tonight," Brigid said to Sheriff Davis as he stepped inside the house. She knew she wasn't the only one who was relieved to see him. Ever since she'd called him, the house seemed to be filled with anxious anticipation. "I know it's getting late and you're off duty, but you could have just sent a deputy or something. I thought I better make a report about what happened."

"Not a problem," he said. He wasn't dressed in his uniform, but he did have his sheriff's department jacket on. "Probably ain't much I can do at the moment, but I felt like we oughta' at least talk 'bout what's going on as soon as possible. That way I can start makin' calls in the morning. Let's get it outta' the way now so we can get the ball rollin'."

Brigid led him over to the seating area in the great room where Linc and Holly were waiting for them. Linc was seated on the couch, nervously shaking his leg, while Holly sat in one of the armchairs. Wade had to leave because of his curfew, but Holly promised to keep him in the loop about what they found out from the sheriff.

She had her phone nearby, ready to relay what she was told. Wade had been frustrated when he had to leave, but considering how little he got to see Holly as it was, he didn't think it would be very smart to push it and end up getting grounded. That would make it even harder to see her.

"So fill me in on what ya' know," Sheriff Davis said as he took a seat in a nearby armchair. He seemed to settle in, ready to take in the important details.

"I'll let Holly explain," Brigid said as she sat down beside Linc. "She knows more about the technical side of things, and I wouldn't know where to begin. I don't want to tell you something and get it wrong, just because I don't know the facts about how it all works."

As Brigid sat back and listened to Holly recount the sequence of events and what she believed had happened, Brigid wondered what they could do about this. Was there even a way to find out who had hacked the website when they couldn't log in themselves? It all seemed really beyond her, and she was worried that the sheriff would be as lost as she was.

Linc looked frustrated and ready to take action. The earlier worry seemed to have been replaced by irritation. He was bouncing his leg as if he was ready to spring into action, but instead was forced to sit and wait. And if he was ready to do something, Brigid couldn't blame him.

Whoever had done this was really petty. What kind of a person would do something like this? There was absolutely no reason to do it. Linc hadn't done anything to cause something like this to happen. Brigid knew him well enough to know he had a heart of gold and would never try to hurt anyone.

"When I went to show Wade the website, I typed in the address, but it didn't come up. It was like the website never existed," Holly said. "We both tried it on our phones as well, thinking something was wrong with my computer, but it still didn't work. That's when I started to worry. I feel like this is my fault. Maybe I could have done something differently," she sighed.

"After all, I hadn't really put much in the way of security in the website, but I didn't think I'd have to this early."

"Holly, there's no way this is your fault," Linc said, finally speaking up. "How were you supposed to know some jerk would do something like this to it?"

"He's right," Brigid said gently. "There was no way you could have known."

"Well, y'all know what my first question's gonna' be," Sheriff Davis said. "Can ya' think of anyone who may have wanted to stop ya' guys from openin' yer' B & B? Anyone been against it from the git-go or might benefit from it not openin'?" the sheriff asked as he pulled out his notebook. "This looks to me like someone's tryin' to stop ya' from openin'."

"I can't think of anyone," Brigid said with a sigh. "I mean, what motivation could there be?"

"Rich Jennings owns the other B & B in town," he pointed out. "How did he feel 'bout ya' guys openin' one?"

Linc jerked his head as though he'd been slapped. "Rich is the one who suggested it," he said softly, his surprise apparent on his face. "I'd never have even thought about opening our own B & B if it hadn't been for him."

"I understand and didn't mean to imply ya' was in the wrong," Sheriff Davis amended. "It's jes', sometimes in these situations ya'd be surprised at how often the culprit is someone the victim thought was a friend or somethin' like that. Ya' know, someone they could trust. Even so, he may've heard somethin' through the grapevine 'bout somebody bein' irritated cuz ya' was gonna' open yer' own place.

"Actually, sometimes ya' can get information 'bout possible suspects jes' by talkin' to other people who are in the same field. I think it'd be wise fer me to pay him a visit in the mornin'." The sheriff made a note to himself in his notebook. "If fer no other reason than to see if he knows of some other B & B that might not be as willin' as he is to share the area with a newbie."

"If you'll let me, I'd like to go with you," Brigid said. "I know it may seem like a conflict of interest, but you know me. I promise I'll keep it professional."

She didn't think it would be possible for her to sit back and wait for others to do the work and see what they come up with. Not when it was Linc's baby. No, she wanted to be out there, helping to dig up clues like she usually did when she'd helped the sheriff in other investigations.

Sheriff Davis took a long look at her, and she briefly wondered if he might say no. Eventually, he sighed. "Probably shouldn't take ya', but I know yer' right. Besides, odd as it may seem, I trust yer' instincts on things like this. Ya' got an ability to see what others aren't sayin' and that's somethin' that jes' can't be taught."

He gave Brigid a nod and she felt a swell of pride sweep over her. She knew the sheriff didn't hand out compliments like that lightly. And he never said things he didn't mean. For him to come out and say something like that was a real treat.

"Can ya' come up with any other possibilities? No matter how much of a stretch?"

"This might be absolutely nothing," Linc began slowly. "But I do think there's someone I may have made angry." His voice indicated he wasn't sure if he should be speaking up, but Brigid was surprised. She hadn't heard anything about this. Why hadn't he told her before now?

"Who?" she asked as she turned toward him.

"There was a guy I approached about doing the website for the B & B," he said with a sigh. "I'll have to look for his name and contact information. He seemed pretty put out when I told him I had my daughter do the website. Maybe I shouldn't have said that, but it never occurred to me that would be a problem. I just thought it was really cool and maybe he'd think it was too. When I told him that, his manner changed. I could tell the guy wasn't happy about it. Even over the phone, I could almost feel the tension in the air after I said I wouldn't be needing his services."

Brigid knew Linc well enough to know he never would have told the guy about Holly to rub it in his face. He was just genuinely proud of her. Knowing Linc, she was sure he'd said it an offhand way and that could have irritated the guy even more, particularly since he probably felt Holly had kept him from a job. She knew people were never happy when you messed with their money.

"Was this a local guy or what?" Sheriff Davis asked.

"Yes, he was," Linc said. "I remember being surprised to find someone here in town who built websites. But he was going to charge me way more than I was comfortable paying, even though it was probably the going rate. After all, the guy is a pro and creates custom websites. I get that, but with all the money we've already spent, I didn't want to go too crazy on it.

"Especially when I knew Holly could do the job, and I trust her. Then she ended up doing a better job than anyone else ever could have done." He shrugged, as if that was explanation enough, which it was, at least to Brigid.

Brigid and Linc looked over at Holly who was furiously typing on her phone. She was too distracted to even notice they were staring at her. Brigid turned away, assuming she was relaying everything to Wade over the phone.

"That's an interestin' thought," Sheriff Davis began as he tapped his pen on his chin. "Holly," he said, turning towards her. She looked up from her phone, surprised.

"Yes?" she asked as she set it down.

"How many people know ya' made the website for the B & B?" he asked.

"I'm not really sure," she said as she looked at the three of them. "Quite a few, I suppose. Why?"

"I was jes' thinkin' that when it comes to somethin' like this, could be that the actual target wasn't the B & B itself. Maybe it was her reputation or Linc's," he said thoughtfully. "I dunno. Jes' me thinkin' out loud."

"So there could be a number of motives for why someone would try to block the website," Brigid said, making sure she was clear on the sheriff's line of thinking.

"It's always possible," he said with a shrug. "If Linc has been braggin' about the website or if someone thought Holly was gettin' too much attention for buildin' it, they mighta' wanted it removed."

Sheriff Davis sat in his chair, seemingly deep in thought and then he said, "Obviously, I don't know anythin' fer sure, but I think ya' guys need to come up with a list of some possible suspects. I'll do a little pokin' around and try to see if there's a way to find out who's been messin' with the website.

"We ain't big enough to have a cyber-crimes unit here in Cottonwood Springs, so I'm gonna' have to ask around." He stood and stretched his back. "Lemme know what ya' come up with tomorrow mornin'. I'm sure I'll have more details then. Think we all need to give this some more thought. We'll pow-wow tomorrow."

As Linc stood up to walk the sheriff to the door, Brigid realized he was right. What they needed was some computer genius who knew how to track someone's digital footprint. She'd heard about that sort of thing, but had no idea who could or would understand what it required. But at least it was somewhere to start.

It was really important to get the website up and running for the grand opening. If they didn't, things were going to be off to a rough start for the New Dawn B & B. Without a website, it would be awfully hard to let potential guests know about the B & B and reserve a room. She knew there was a very real possibility that their grand adventure to open their own B & B might just be over before it even started.

CHAPTER TWELVE

The next morning at breakfast, everyone was in a glum mood even though Linc had fried some sausage links, eggs, and made toast. No one spoke as Holly, Linc, and Brigid stayed lost in their own thoughts, trying to piece things together. Like how in the world any of this had happened and what they could do about it? But none of them were feeling very hopeful that there was anything they could do about the situation.

"I had an idea," Holly began after taking a few sips of juice and eating her toast. "It's a long shot, but I know someone I think might be able to help. She's far more into technology than I am. I wanted to check with you two first to make sure you didn't mind me telling someone what's going on. I thought maybe you'd want to keep it hush-hush or something."

Brigid looked over at Linc, who shrugged. She turned back to Holly and said, "We don't mind. If you think someone can help, feel free to reach out to them. I think in this situation we can use all the help we can get. Who do you have in mind?" she asked as she took a bite of a sausage link and listened to Holly.

"Her name is Vega. She's really great with computers and even built her own. She's known in school as being the go-to person if you're having tech problems. She has a little business replacing cell phone screens and has written her own programs and apps. She's like a computer genius. I thought if we could figure out how this happened, it might help us find out who did it."

"I hope she can help," Brigid nodded. "Especially since what Sheriff Davis said is right. I really doubt that there are a lot of local people who could help us with this sort of thing. We almost need someone capable of taking down a website so we can know what actually happened."

Brigid had been thinking about that very fact during most of the night. Tossing and turning in bed, she'd wondered how they were going to find out who had done it. As far as she knew, there was no way to trace it.

"I'll see if I can get ahold of her after I finish breakfast. She's a busy girl, so it might take some time," Holly explained.

"If you can work with her and then we work with the sheriff, maybe we can end up combining our information and find out who did it," Linc suggested. "There's no reason why we can't try a couple of different approaches and see what we come up with."

"Okay, I'll see what I can do," Holly said happily. Brigid knew she enjoyed helping out when she could. If anything, Holly liked solving mysteries as much as Brigid did.

"I'll try to find the information for that web developer," Linc said. "I know I have it somewhere on my computer."

"You do that and try to think if there's anyone else," Brigid said. "I'll head over to the sheriff's department and see what he's found. If either one of you turns anything up, let me know." She finished her breakfast and stood up to take her plate to the sink.

"I hope we find out whoever did this soon," Holly said as she took the last bite of her breakfast. "I hate the thought that they think they can do something like this and get away with it."

"They aren't going to get away with it," Brigid vowed as she turned away from the sink. "We will find whoever did this. Some way, some how. We just have to use our heads, work together, and stay positive."

"I'm trying," Linc sighed. "But I'm with Holly. This seems a little out of our league."

"That's why we reach out," Brigid said decisively. "You two do your thing. I'm going to stop by the bookstore and tell Fiona what's happening. I told her a little of what was going on when I texted her this morning, but it was too much information to put in a text. I promised I'd swing by really quick before going to see Sheriff Davis."

"Sounds good," Linc said as he stood up. "Give me a kiss, I'm going to go do my thing too."

Twenty minutes later, Brigid was pulling up in front of her sister's bookstore. It seemed as though it had been far too long since she'd been there and it was just Fiona working at the shop. It brought back memories of the days just after she'd moved back home to Cottonwood Springs.

The little bell over the door rang out pleasantly as she stepped inside the bookstore. Fiona looked up from her spot in the corner where she was reading. "Hey," she said with a smile. "How's it going?"

"Not so hot," Brigid sighed. "Where's Aiden?"

"He's asleep in the back," she said as she lifted a baby monitor and showed it to Brigid. "It's quieter back there, so he naps longer."

"That's smart," Brigid said as she walked across the store and sat down across from her sister.

"Tell me what's going on with the website," Fiona said. "You texted me that it's gone. Is it?"

"Something like that," Brigid nodded as she turned in her chair to get more comfortable. "It looks like someone hacked into our website and took it down. Completely. Holly can't log into it at all. She said it's like it's there, but it's not, which I'm not sure I fully understand."

"Darn," Fiona said, surprised. "Why would someone do that?"

"Absolutely no idea," Brigid admitted. "We have a bunch of theories, but nothing concrete." And it frustrated her that she had no idea why it had happened. It would be so much easier if she knew why someone had targeted them.

"What are the theories?" Fiona asked as she cocked her head to one side.

Brigid explained to Fiona all the different theories they'd come up with for why someone might take down their website. From being angry about a new B & B to Linc or Holly having made someone mad. She outlined everything they'd brainstormed about the situation, hoping her sister might be able to help her fill in some blanks.

"Seriously, you guys think someone could have it in for Holly and did this out of spite to her?" Fiona asked, astonished.

Brigid shrugged. "At this point we really have no clue. It could be any one of those things or none of them. Heck, as far as we know, it could just be some random person who decided they wanted to take it down just because."

"That seems like a stretch, though," Fiona said as she shook her head.

"Yeah, but is it?" Brigid asked. "Think about all those people who like to hack into people's social media accounts. And for what? I'm learning it's a crazy world online. People seem desensitized to the fact that there's another person on the other end of the screen. It's almost as if they think they aren't hurting anyone by their actions."

"That's very true," Fiona admitted. "But I'm having a hard time imagining anyone disliking Holly that much," she sighed.

"Who knows?" Brigid said with a shrug. "We have to look at all the possibilities." They lapsed into silence as Brigid continued to think about the situation. She thought the idea that someone had done it because they had disliked Holly was a stretch.

If she had to guess, she thought it was probably someone who didn't want the B & B to open. Maybe it was someone in a nearby town who didn't like the idea. Her mind jumped to Rich Jennings, but she pushed that thought away immediately. She just couldn't imagine it being him. Not in a million years.

"I had a talk with Abra last night," Fiona began.

"Oh?" Brigid asked. She wasn't really sure where her sister was going with this, but she hoped it wasn't about their parents again.

"I did," Fiona said carefully. She stood and walked over to the coffee pot. "You want a cup?" she asked as she held the carafe up.

"No thanks," Brigid said. "And?"

"And she feels as though she needs to talk to you. She said it's like a strong urge that she can't shake. She said she felt it when she met you, but she sensed you didn't really want to talk to her." Fiona gave her sister a pointed look that almost seemed to be chastising her.

"It wasn't that," Brigid sighed. "You know how I am."

"I do," Fiona said as she poured herself a cup of coffee and turned around. "I also know that you can be pretty stand-offish and maybe even a little rude if you don't want to talk."

"Can you blame me?" Brigid asked, feeling a little ruffled.

"Not at all," Fiona said, doing her best to calm her sister. "But Abra doesn't like to push issues, even when they need to be pushed.

I'm telling you, she's got this feeling for a reason, and you need to hear her out. She'll be coming in soon if you want to stick around."

"I'm not trying to be rude to her," Brigid explained. "I just don't want to talk about our parents with someone I don't even know." She didn't tell her that she was a little afraid of the woman. She didn't want Abra bringing something up that no one else knew. There was one conversation she'd had in particular that she'd rather forget ever happened. And the fact that no one else alive was aware of that conversation made it a lot easier for her to do.

"I get it," Fiona said softly as she returned to her seat. "Really, I do. But you should still think about it. I know how you are. If you just have time to think about it for a while, you'll be a lot more receptive. That's why I've been telling you about her. I want you to get used to the idea.

"I know you've got some serious baggage that you still carry around when it comes to our parents. I don't want you to feel pushed to do anything you don't want to do, but I think it's been long enough. Whatever it is that you think you did wrong, it doesn't matter anymore."

"Well, maybe it still matters to me," Brigid said as her throat tightened. "Maybe I'm still not ready."

"Sometimes you'll never be ready to do something, and you just have to jump," Fiona said. "You have to let go and trust that someone will catch you if you fall. You know I'll always be here for you, right? There's nothing you could tell me that would make me think less of you."

Brigid wasn't so sure about that, but she wasn't going to argue the point. If she did, it would just cause Fiona to probe more. As it was, she needed to get out of the bookstore before Abra showed up.

"I know," Brigid said as she forced a smile on her face. She pulled out her phone and looked at the time. "Well, I better go. Sheriff Davis will be waiting on me. We're having a meeting to discuss the website stuff. He's helping me try to find out who did it."

"Good luck," Fiona said. "I hope you figure something out. I'd hate to see all that hard work, to say nothing of the expense, go down the drain."

"Me, too," Brigid said as she headed for the door. "Me, too."

CHAPTER THIRTEEN

Brigid almost felt badly about leaving Fiona's bookstore in such a hurry. She knew her sister was just trying to be helpful, but she didn't seem to really appreciate the fact that Brigid did not want to talk about it. Didn't Fiona think she was entitled to that? Couldn't there be things she simply never wanted to talk about? She was sure there were things that other people never wanted to talk about. Why couldn't she be the same?

As she drove her car the short distance from the bookstore to the sheriff's department, she pushed the whole thing to the back of her mind. Right now, she didn't need to think about it. She had a case to focus on, a case that was very personal to her. Somehow, she needed to figure out who had taken down the website and get it back online. That was her number one priority. Everything else had to take a backseat to it.

She knew Linc would be a huge ball of stress until it was back up and running, so there was no way she could worry about anything else until then. When Linc was stressed, he cooked. If she didn't find out what had happened and fix it, she knew within a day there would be way too much food for three people to eat.

"Hey, Brigid. Good to see ya'," Sheriff Davis said as she stepped inside the sheriff's station. "Come on back. We can talk in my office."

The sheriff's station looked the same as ever. A long wooden counter separated the deputies' desks from the front of the room. At the back was a door and that led to Sheriff Davis' office. Beyond that was a hallway that led to the holding cells and other rooms, such as the evidence room and the locker room. Brigid didn't go back there much. More often than not, when she came to the sheriff's station, it was to talk to the sheriff, and that always took place in his office.

Brigid waved at a couple of the deputies as she walked back to his office. It was nice to be accepted by the rest of the department, considering she wasn't considered much more than a consultant. But they all seemed to appreciate the fact that she was simply very good at helping them out. In between her own cases, there were always a couple who would ask her opinion about whatever they were working on.

"Hi, Brigid," Deputy Keegan said, as she appeared from the hallway. "How are you today?"

"Could be better," Brigid admitted. "But once I find the bad guy, I'll feel just fine."

"I'm sure you will," Deputy Keegan said with a smile. "Let me know if you need my help. I'd love a distraction from my boring paperwork."

"Will do," Brigid said as she continued to walk towards the sheriff's office.

She stepped into it and sat down. Sheriff Davis shut the door behind her before making his way around his desk and sitting down with a groan. "Well, I guess I'll go first. 'Fraid what I found isn't that greata' news. I can get someone who specializes in cyber-crimes to take a look at the case, but jes' like I was afraid of, it's gonna' take some time."

"How much time?" Brigid asked. She, too, had been worried about that. She'd wondered just how far away Sheriff Davis would have to call to find someone who worked on cyber-crimes. And she guessed the farther out he had to reach, the longer it would probably take. After all, other places would also be turning to them with their problems.

"They tol' me it would be at least two weeks, if not more," he said, looking regretful. "They said if I need to get on the list, I better do it right away. I guess cyber-crimes are getting more and more popular, but they ain't got many people yet that specialize in that sorta' thing."

"That's not going to work," Brigid said shaking her head. "We need that website up and running sooner than that."

"I know," Sheriff Davis said. "I talked to Rich this morning. I didn't tell him I was concerned he may be a suspect. Instead, I told him we needed a little information from him. He said to swing by any time after 10:00 this mornin'."

"Good," Brigid said. "Holly and I were talking this morning, and she said she knows a student who might know enough about computers to help us out," she explained. "She's going to try to get in contact with her today and see if she'd be willing to help us."

"It would be great if she could," Sheriff Davis said. "I know time is of the essence. I'd like to see this taken care of and be over with cuz' y'all have a business to get runnin', and I don't want anythin' to get in the way of that. I consider you and Linc my friends. Matter of fact, many times as I've had dinner at your place, yer' almost family.

"I can't stand the thought that someone did this to ya', and I'm ready to catch 'em and clean this up. Which reminds me, is this gonna' be an official thing? Ya' gonna' want to press charges against whoever did this? After all, if this takes very long and the B & B doesn't open on time, what they did will probably cost ya' some bucks."

"I'm not really sure," Brigid said. "If it was an accident, I don't really see the need to press charges. But if it was malicious, then that's another story."

Sheriff Davis nodded and sucked on his teeth. "Yeah, that's what I was thinkin' you'd say. Fer now, I'm going to treat it like any other crime. Once we know more about it ya' can decide what direction ya' want to take with it. That work fer ya'?"

"Yes, Corey, and I really appreciate it," Brigid said. "I just can't say for sure until I know what happened. Maybe whoever did this didn't intend for it to go like this. I need to know what the intent was."

"Then I reckon that means we should get to it. It's after 10:00, so let's head on over to visit Rich. If anythin', maybe he can give us some other ideas 'bout it," he said as he stood and put his on his hat.

Brigid stood up and followed him out of the building and over to his truck. She climbed into the passenger seat and buckled up before he pulled away and they headed towards Rich's B & B.

"Ya' think this is gonna affect yer' business?" Sheriff Davis asked as he drove.

"I'm not really sure at this point," Brigid said. "In the grand scheme of things, probably not as much as we might think. After all, what would another week or so matter? But considering Linc has already been worried about every little minor detail, this is really stressing him."

"Understandable," Sheriff Davis said. "He wants to make a good impression. Get off on the right foot and all of that. Can't blame him. In this day and age, seems that's mighty important."

"Yes, it is," Brigid agreed. "Which may be why someone did this in the first place."

"Ya' got it," Sheriff Davis said as they came into sight of the B & B. Rich had left everything just as it had been when his sister had run it. The outside was a simple but neat appearing home, while on the inside it was filled with history.

His parents, the ones who had opened the B & B, had been big lovers of local history and even had a few Native American artifacts on display. Rich knew many of the nearby historical spots and often pointed his visitors in their direction if they were interested.

Rich was sitting on a wicker couch that was on the large front porch, reading the paper. "Good morning," he called as they climbed out of the truck and shut the doors.

"Mornin' Rich," Sheriff Davis answered. "Good to see ya'. How ya' been?" he asked as Rich climbed down the stairs that led off the side of the porch.

"Right as rain," Rich said with a smile. "Brigid, it's good to see you," he said, still grinning.

"I'm glad to see you too," she said as they followed him up the stairs to the porch.

"I thought we could visit out here in the fresh air, if that's alright with you. Do either of you want some coffee or a glass of water?" Rich asked as he gestured for them to take a seat on one of the nearby chairs.

"I don't need anything," Brigid said.

"Me neither and outside is jes' fine by me," Sheriff Davis said. "I get enough indoor air being stuck in the office."

"I well remember, and not fondly," Rich said with a chuckle. "You said you had some sort of issue you thought I might be able to help with?" he said.

"We do," Sheriff Davis said, nodding. "Appears someone hacked into Brigid and Linc's new B & B website and took it down."

He left it at that, watching the other man to see what his reaction might be. Brigid's initial instinct was that Rich wasn't the hacker type, but then again, people could surprise you. He was a smart man, and the internet was full of information. She didn't know what it would require to get into someone's website, but if there was a tutorial or something online, he or anyone else could probably have followed it.

"Is that so?" Rich asked as he turned to Brigid, his eyes filled with sympathy. "How can I help?"

"We're at a complete loss as to who would do this to us," Brigid explained. "We thought maybe you could help us look in the right direction."

"Hmm," he said as he leaned forward and cradled his chin in his hand. "Well, I'm not really sure. I don't...," but then he paused. "Wait a minute. I may actually know something that might be of help," he said wagging his finger at them. "It was online and vague, but I bet you could be who they were talking about."

"What was it?" Brigid asked.

"There's this group online. It's private and for B & B owners only. Kind of a place where we can complain together and whatnot," he explained. "I don't know why I didn't connect the dots before." He shook his head in frustration.

"Anyway, this one woman who posts occasionally recently posted complaining about a new B & B opening up near her. She went on to say she was in New Haven, Colorado, which piqued my curiosity, since that's so close to Cottonwood Springs.

"The woman said she saw their amazing website, and she wished she could find a way to take it down. She didn't think it was fair that this B & B had such a nice website when they were just starting out. Basically, she was looking for sympathy, but I'll bet she was talking about your B & B. After all, I don't know of any other B & B's in the area so close to opening that they have websites up." He looked from Brigid to Sheriff Davis.

"Interesting," Brigid said. She and Linc had done their research on where all the local B & B's were, and she knew of one in New Haven.

"As I recall, she has the only B & B in town. We wanted to make a list and talk to all of them about mutual referrals," she explained.

"You mean like everyone helping out if they can? That's a good idea. Refer to someone not too far away when you're booked up," Rich nodded. "I'd at least give her a call," he shrugged. "I mean, it's public record she said that. I can go in and get screenshots and send them over to you, if that would help."

"Appreciate it if ya' did," Sheriff Davis said. "Jes' in case it turns into something. And if this woman's the only B & B in New Haven, shouldn't be that hard to find her and have a polite conversation. Whaddya' think, Brigid?"

"I'm up for it," she agreed. There was no way she'd be able to relax until she found out who did this, anyway. Once she started an investigation, she preferred to focus completely on it.

"Rich, what kinda' person ya' think would do somethin' like this?" Sheriff Davis asked. "Ya' had some great instincts when ya' were in my position. Value any input ya' can give me on this."

"Well, if I didn't know me, I'd wonder about myself." He turned to Brigid and gave her a kind smile. "I wouldn't blame you if I'd been on your list, but I thank you for not coming out and asking. I think it speaks of your trust in me."

Brigid smiled and nodded. "Of course. But you were still the best person to ask first anyway."

"That I was," he agreed. "I just wish I knew more than I do, but at least it's a start for you. These online things can make stuff tricky. I wish you all the best of luck. Let me know if you decide to go through with contacting the other B & B's. I'd be more than happy to do what I can. I've made a few friends online that could help make it a larger scale thing."

"Great," Brigid said as she and the sheriff stood up. "Thank you for your time."

"Good luck, and I hope you figure out who did it. I'd say it would take someone with some real skills behind a computer. As good as the younger generation is, might want to look there." Rich started rubbing his chin as he thought it, but he had nothing more to say.

Brigid remembered what the sheriff had said about someone doing this because of a grudge they may have had against Holly, and a chill ran down her back. She really hoped that wasn't the case.

CHAPTER FOURTEEN

As Sheriff Davis and Brigid climbed back into the truck, Brigid wondered if New Haven was in the sheriff's jurisdiction. She looked over at him and thought about saying something about it, but decided against it. She trusted that he knew what he was doing, and she knew there was no way he'd do something that was illegal. She settled back and prepared for the short ride to New Haven.

"I'll look up the address for the B & B in New Haven," she said as she pulled out her phone.

"Good. Think I may know where it's at, but I'd rather be certain than waste time," Sheriff Davis said as they left Cottonwood Springs.

Brigid easily found the address and pulled it up on the GPS on her phone. She and the sheriff chatted about any and everything as he drove towards New Haven. In their time working together, they'd become good friends who looked out for each other and gave advice when it was needed.

"So how are things going between you and Deputy Keegan?" she asked.

The sheriff glanced over at her like he considered arguing once again that there wasn't anything going on, but seemed to think better of it. "We're tryin' to keep things perfessional," he said simply.

"I see," Brigid said with a nod. "And how's that going?"

"'Bout as well as you could expect. I really like her, but we're in a bit of a predicament with me bein' her boss and all," he said.

"I'm sure," Brigid nodded. "And you both like where you are, so neither of you wants to change things. Well, I wish you both the best." And she did. She understood they were in a tight spot, but feelings had a way of cropping up when you least expect them.

"Thanks," he said. They continued to chat until they were in New Haven. The B & B they were looking for was right on the edge of town. It was an older farm house with a long driveway and a white fence on either side of it. Chickens were roaming the yard, in search of bugs and anything else they could find.

"Oh, I never thought about getting chickens," Brigid cooed as they pulled up.

"Ya' live inside the city limits, Brigid. Hate to say it, but they ain't allowed," he said somewhat apologetically as he shut off his truck.

"Well, darn," she said. There were two vehicles parked nearby and Brigid wondered if the owner might have a guest. Rich had sent them the information about the owner of the New Haven B & B. They knew her name was Nora Russo and that she'd been working hard at building up her B & B. They also had her screen name from the group and a few other posts that Rich had thought might be referring to Linc and Brigid's B & B. Papers in hand, they walked up to the porch.

"Good morning," a woman called out cheerfully as she pushed open the screen door and stepped outside. She was wearing an apron and dried her hands on it. "How can I help you?"

"Are you Nora Russo?" Sheriff Davis asked.

"I sure am," she said with a grin.

"I'm Sheriff Davis and this is Brigid Olsen. We're here to ask ya' a few questions, if you ain't too busy?" the sheriff said.

"Not at all. I was just making some bread. You're welcome to come in and sit. Ask away, if you don't mind me still working on my bread," Nora said cheerfully.

"That's not a problem, ma'am," Sheriff Davis said as Nora turned and led them into the B & B.

Inside was exactly what Brigid expected. It looked like a traditional farmhouse with hardwood floors, flowers everywhere, and white paneling on the lower half of the walls with a chair rail dividing it from the sunflower yellow painted walls above it. Nora led them to the open kitchen where there were bar stools on the outside of a counter that had flour and dough spread across it.

"Please, take a seat. Can I get you anything? I have some fresh-squeezed lemonade." she said, smiling.

"No, thank ya', Ms. Russo. We promise not to take up too much of yer' time, so I'll jes' cut to the chase," Sheriff Davis said. "A local B & B owner has been havin' a few issues regardin' their website and it looks like it was done intentionally. Unfortunately, ya' made some remarks in a certain group about a local B & B and how you wished somethin' would happen to their website." He gave her a pointed look and she froze, her hands hovering over the bread.

"What do you mean, something's happened?" she asked. She looked stricken, as if she couldn't believe it.

"Their website was completely removed from the internet by someone," Brigid supplied as she typed in the web address on her phone and showed Nora the empty screen.

"Oh, no," she said, sounding horrified. She looked from Brigid to the sheriff. "I admit to saying those things. There's no point in denying it. You wouldn't be here if you weren't sure I'd done that. But I didn't do anything to their website, I promise. I was just blowing smoke, you know? I was angry and frustrated, but I'd never do anything like that."

"We got a computer expert lookin' into it now," Sheriff Davis began. Brigid knew he was bluffing, but she nodded along to prove his point. "They're trackin' down the IP address that did this. If ya' had somethin' to do with this, sure would be better to tell us now."

"I wouldn't lie," Nora said as she shook her head. "When did this happen?"

"Last night," Brigid said. "And I should tell you I'm one of the owners of the New Dawn B & B in Cottonwood Springs."

Nora paused and seemed to really look at Brigid. "That's where I've seen you before. I was wondering because you look so familiar. I'm sorry I wrote what I did, but I didn't do anything to your website. That's pretty low."

Brigid watched the woman as she spoke, but didn't get the feeling the woman was trying to lie to her. She seemed genuinely surprised about it. Brigid nodded. "I had intentions of contacting the local B & B's to set something up with everyone. My husband and I had discussed referring any extra guests we might have to other nearby B & B's.

"You know, kind of a good faith connection between all of us. After all, each of us only has so many rooms. If we work together, we can try and make sure that everyone is doing well, so no one has to feel as though their business is threatened." She looked around approvingly. "You have a very nice place here. I would have no trouble sending people to your B & B. It seems so quiet and relaxing here."

"Really? That's a great idea," Nora said happily. "I'd love to do that. Not that I've been full yet, but if I was, that wouldn't be a problem. I'd much rather work together. Say, who built your website anyway? I did mine myself, and it's a bit lacking." She turned back to her bread now that the tension was gone.

"Actually, my daughter did it," Brigid said. "And one of her friends took the photos."

"You're kidding?" she said, clearly stunned. "Do you think she would do a website for me?"

"Perhaps. I can let her know you're interested," Brigid said. "But I have to tell you, she's already starting to get fairly popular."

"Please do. I don't have much to pay her, but I'll do my best to pay whatever she's asking," Nora said with a nod.

"Ya' got a number we can reach ya' at in case we got more questions?" Sheriff Davis asked. "Considerin' this is an ongoin' investigation, we'd appreciate all the help we can get."

"Oh, sure," she said as she hurried over to the fireplace in the nearby living room where she had a stack of business cards. "Here's a couple of cards. Please give one to your daughter." She handed one to Brigid. "And please keep me updated on your idea for all of us to help one another,"

"I will," Brigid said, starting to feel better about the woman. "We'll leave you to your bread."

"Thank you, and I hope you find out who did that to your website. It was beautiful, so I hope it gets up and running again," she said as she followed them to the door.

Sheriff Davis and Brigid said their good byes and stepped outside. Once they were a little ways from the house, Sheriff Davis turned around to see if Nora was watching them. When he was sure she wasn't, he turned to Brigid.

"Whaddya' think?" he asked before walking around to his side of the truck.

"I don't know," Brigid admitted after climbing inside. "She doesn't seem like the type, but we'll still keep her in mind."

"Yeah, I agree. She seems more like the type of person to talk a big game than to actually do somethin'. But I still wanna' keep an eye on her. She's got a motive and she's made threats, so I gotta' consider her a solid suspect until we know more." The sheriff started the truck and turned around. "Sure seemed like she wanted Holly to build her a website, though."

"Boy, did she," Brigid said. "I can't believe how popular Holly has gotten because of all of this."

"Yeah," Sheriff Davis said. "And it's making me wonder if the B & B was the target after all."

"It just seems odd for someone to take the website down if their main target was Holly," Brigid said as she shook her head. "It just doesn't fit."

"I know, but I still have a funny feelin' 'bout it all. I think we're gonna' have to get creative with this one," Sheriff Davis said with a sigh as they pulled back out on the road.

Brigid sat silently watching out her window as the landscape went by. If she were to bet, she still would have said Nora did it. But the more she thought about the woman's reaction to what they'd said, it didn't fit. Granted, she could be good at faking it, but that seemed unlikely. Maybe Holly's friend could shed some light on the whole situation. She pulled out her phone to see if she'd missed any calls, but when she looked at the screen, she saw there weren't any.

"Expecting a call?" the sheriff asked.

"Just hoping Holly can get the girl she knows on board to help us. Right now that seems like our best bet to figuring out who did this to our website," Brigid sighed.

"I hope so too. Otherwise this is gonna' be a longer case than I'd like. We gots us a track record of wrappin' things up fairly quickly. Don't want this to be an exception," Sheriff Davis said as he stared at the road.

"Me neither," Brigid said, silently wishing Holly good luck.

CHAPTER FIFTEEN

When the sheriff and Brigid had almost reached the Cottonwood Springs city limits, her phone began to ring. When she answered, she heard Linc's voice.

"I found the web developer's information. He emailed it all to me after our phone conversation, so I'm going to forward it over to you now. His name is Jack Hubbard. He included his address and everything. He told me that he worked from home, so he should be there during the day. Maybe you can stop by his home this morning," he said.

Brigid looked at her phone while she continued to talk and opened the email. She held it up so that Sheriff Davis could see the address and he nodded.

"Okay, we'll head over there in a few minutes," she said. "We're just returning from New Haven where we met with Nora, the woman with the B & B over there. Rich told us this morning that she'd posted some fairly incriminating things online about wanting our website to go down."

Brigid still wasn't 100% sure that it hadn't been her, but out of the people they knew of so far, this Jack guy seemed to have the most expertise to pull something like that off.

"Since you're still looking, I'm going to assume you don't think she did it," he surmised. "Oh, wait. Holly wants to tell you something too," he said before handing the phone to Holly.

"Brigid?" Holly said.

"Yeah, Holly. What's up?" Brigid asked.

"Remember the girl from school I told you about, Vega? She said she'd help and came over here not too long ago. I gave her all the info that she needed and so far, she has one thing for us. She said she's almost certain that whoever did this is right here in town. There was a lot of technical stuff about them possibly using something to mask their location, but she's very doubtful that's the case. She told me to tell you that if it was her, she'd start with anyone you suspect here in town. But it's going to take a little more time," she said.

"We're getting ready to head to the website developer's home," Brigid said. "He's here in Cottonwood Springs, and I'm starting to think he's our best bet." Brigid looked over at the sheriff who shrugged.

"Good luck, I hope it is, and if it is him, see if you can get him to turn the site back over to us. I spent too much time developing that site to have it simply disappear into thin air. It's so frustrating," Holly sighed.

"Speaking of that. I may have another client for you, Holly. The woman in New Haven we just talked to wants you to build a site for her. You might want to start thinking about how much you're going to charge," Brigid said proudly.

It was nice that Holly was getting recognized for all her hard work. As long as she kept her grades up, in addition to working at Fiona's bookstore, she could get a nice little side business going. Not bad for a high school girl.

"I will. Talk to you soon," Holly said before she ended the call.

"So ya' think this next guy's our culprit, huh?" Sheriff Davis asked.

Brigid sighed. "I'm not sure. But you heard what Holly said. That girl Vega says the suspect lives right here in town. At this point, who else could it be?" Brigid couldn't imagine anyone else who would want to take down their website. Losing business to a kid could make a man angry enough to do something like hack into the website, or so she thought.

"I hear ya'," Sheriff Davis said. "And I hope yer' right. Still, let's keep our minds open. Don't know if we've got all the pieces to the puzzle lined up just yet. She said that girl's still workin' on it?"

"She is. Hopefully, she'll give us what we need," Brigid said. "It would really help to have something concrete, since I feel completely out of my comfort zone. There's no crime scene to look at or evidence to speak of. Just a missing website."

"I hear ya'. Digital stuff makes me real nervous. I hope we don't start havin' more cases like this," he sighed as he shook his head. "I think this is the place." They pulled up in front of a one-story home that was mostly red brick with black shutters. It was neatly kept up and the yard was well taken care of, not exactly the type of house where Brigid imagined a criminal would live. Still, most criminals didn't put signs in their yard letting you know they couldn't be trusted.

As she got out of the truck, Brigid took a deep breath and hoped this was the break they needed. Even if this guy wasn't who they were looking for, Brigid silently hoped he'd be able to give them some direction as to where they should go with the investigation. Otherwise, they were going to be at a dead end unless Holly's friend, Vega, came up with something else.

When they approached the front door, Sheriff Davis pushed the doorbell and stood back.

"Here we go," he said quietly to her. Within a few moments, the door opened and a man in his late twenties or early thirties stood there.

"May I help you?" he asked, clearly concerned to see that there was a sheriff standing on his porch.

"Are ya' Jack Hubbard?" Sheriff Davis asked.

"Yes, sir," Jack said. His eyes darted from Brigid to the sheriff and back again.

"We got a few questions for ya', if ya' don't mind. I'm Sheriff Davis with the Cottonwood Springs Sheriff's department and this here is Brigid Olsen, my consultant," he said sounding extremely formal. His tone almost surprised Brigid.

"Yes, sir. Please come in," he said as he held the door open.

Stepping inside, they saw that most of the furniture had seen better days. There were a few newer items here and there, but the couch and recliner looked like something Brigid would expect in an older person's home.

"The house used to be my grandparents' home," Jack explained. "I didn't have the money for all new furniture, so some of it's a little dated." He gestured to the couch and sat down in the recliner.

"Mr. Hubbard, can ya' tell me what you do fer a livin'?" Sheriff Davis asked.

"I'm a website developer," Jack said proudly. "I build websites for people all across the country."

"That's interestin'," Sheriff Davis said. "Does that mean ya' can also get into other people's websites?" he asked.

"I'm not really sure," Jack said, slightly taken aback. "I guess theoretically I could if I had their login information."

"But what if ya' didn't?" Sheriff Davis asked.

"I'm not sure what you're saying," Jack said, shaking his head.

"A local business had their website hacked," Brigid interrupted. "We're trying to find out who did it. Right now, you're looking pretty good for it."

"Seriously?" Jack asked. "How could I? Why would I? That's ridiculous!" he leaned back in his chair, completely flummoxed.

"Is it?" Sheriff Davis asked. "Because I got a tech person on it right now who says that whoever did it lives right here in Cottonwood Springs. Since ya' were pretty mad Linc Olsen had his daughter build his site fer him instead of you, I'm wonderin' if ya' decided to take matters into yer' own hands."

"I didn't, I swear. When did this happen?" Jack asked, worried.

"Last night," Brigid said. "And I'm one of the owners."

"Oh," Jack said, stunned for a moment. "But I wasn't even here. I was in Denver visiting my parents. I drove home this morning. I wasn't even in Cottonwood Springs last night."

"I see," Sheriff Davis said as he seemed to study the man. "I hope yer' not lyin' to us."

"I'm not, trust me. When your tech person is finished, they'll tell you. It wasn't my IP address. My digital fingerprints will be nowhere near your website," he said as he looked at Brigid.

Brigid wanted it to be him. She really did. But looking into the man's eyes, all she saw was fear. There was no deceit or any other emotion that hinted he was hiding something.

"Okay," she said. "But do understand this is an ongoing investigation. We still may need to speak with you."

"That's not a problem," Jack said. "If there's anything I can do to help, let me know. I took a course on ethical hacking once. I'm not sure what I remember, but I'd do my best to help."

"Ethical hackin'?" Sheriff Davis asked, confused. "Them two words sure sound like they don't go together to me."

Jack chuckled. "You wouldn't think. But there are people who are paid to hack into things in order to test security. Big companies often hire those types of people to test their own security measures to make sure the bad hackers can't get in. I've considered going into it, but I'd have to take a few more classes first."

"I see," Sheriff Davis said. "I may still be in touch with ya', but gotta' tell ya', I appreciate yer' honesty."

"Anything I can do to help, let me know. And I admit, I was frustrated when I saw your website," Jack confessed. "Your daughter did an excellent job. She could definitely have a future in website development if she's interested. These days, you don't even need to go to college for it. You just need to show you have what it takes, and from what I saw, she seems to."

"Thanks, I'll tell her," Brigid said. She was glad it wasn't Jack. He seemed like an honest guy just trying to make a living. Who could blame him for being frustrated that someone had taken business away from him? Brigid could relate to that. It was just human nature to have that sort of a reaction. Working for yourself was no cakewalk. Not when you're building something from the ground up on your own.

"If she has any questions, tell her she can send me a message. I'm easy to find online," he added.

Sheriff Davis stood up and Brigid followed. "We better go. We got more investigatin' to do," he said gruffly. Jack nodded and shook each of their hands before they left his home and climbed back in the truck.

"Well that sure didn't amount to a hill of beans," Sheriff Davis grumbled. "Sorry, Brigid."

"Sorry for what?" she asked. Brigid had no clue why he would be apologizing to her.

"Fer not findin' who did this," he sighed as he turned the key in the truck's ignition. "I'm jes' not seein' a way thru this one."

"We'll find it," she said confidently. "Once we get back to the station, I'll go home and see if Holly's friend has come up with anything else. Maybe there's something we're missing. It could be someone who's upset with Holly or Linc, and we just haven't thought about them. It might just take a little more digging, that's all."

"I hope yer' right," he said as he started to drive back towards the station.

CHAPTER SIXTEEN

Brigid pulled in her driveway, a little sad that she didn't have good news for Linc. She knew Sheriff Davis was right when he said they usually did manage to figure things out a little quicker than this. Or at least have some vague idea who it may be. There would be a list of suspects that they slowly would cross off until they were left with the culprit. Then, they could round them up and make the arrest. But not this time.

However, at this point, she had nothing to offer. No more clues and no more suspects. It was disappointing, to say the least. The idea of having to walk into her house and tell Linc she didn't have any more leads was making her linger in her car a little longer than she normally did.

Brigid was hoping if she sat there long enough, a brilliant idea might come to her. Yet try as she might, nothing came to mind. She didn't have a single brilliant revelation or bright idea. Nothing. She knew she had to get out of the car pretty soon or Linc and Holly might think something was wrong. She was sure they'd heard her pull up and stop outside.

She got out of her car, collected her purse, and headed for the front door with a heavy heart. She looked up when she heard the door open.

"Brigid, I'm so glad you're home," Holly said as she opened the front door. She looked happy to see Brigid, probably assuming that she and the sheriff had figured out who did it. The thought of having to make that glad expression fall from Holly's face hurt Brigid more than a little bit.

"We didn't find who did it," Brigid said softly. "I'm at a dead end for now." She shook her head as she crossed the driveway. If only there was something else to do.

"Well, we aren't," Holly said. "We have a lead, but I have to talk to you first." She shut the door behind her and jogged down the steps of the porch, her blonde hair bouncing behind her.

"Okay, about what?" Brigid asked, concerned. She was so distracted by disappointing Holly it hadn't really registered that Holly had said they had a lead.

"Vega has something to tell you, but she's a little worried she might get in trouble," Holly explained. "You need to reassure her that she won't."

"Oh?" Brigid said. "What kind of trouble?" Brigid wasn't quite sure what kind of trouble this girl could possibly get in. And how in the world could she get in trouble about something having to do with the website?

"She needs to know you won't hold it against her. She really didn't mean any harm. I don't want to tell you the details, because that's up to her. But just know she didn't even really think about the effect of what she was doing might have," Holly said pointedly. "It has to do with the website."

"Alright," Brigid nodded. "I'll definitely keep that in mind. Am I going to get upset?" She felt that if she was prepared, she could work out a way to process it before she had to hear it from Vega.

"I don't really think so, just hear her out," Holly shrugged as she looped her arm through Brigid's and led her to the door. "Otherwise, how was your day? Was it good besides all of that?"

"Not super great," Brigid sighed as she opened the front door. "I'd feel much better if I had a lead or some sort of idea what to do next. I'm not used to this feeling."

"Don't worry about it," Holly said touching her arm. "Vega has that part covered." She gestured towards the girl who was leaning over a laptop at a coffee table in the great room. She was Hispanic with beautiful long dark hair that was tucked behind her ears. Glasses were perched on the end of her nose as she peered down at the screen. She looked up and smiled nervously.

"Hi, Mrs. Olsen," she said softly.

"Please, call me Brigid," Brigid said kindly. She moved to the table where the girl was sitting and pulled up a chair. From her position at the table, she could see Linc moving around the kitchen as he cooked. He gave her a little smile.

"Brigid, I need to tell you something," Vega said with a sigh as Holly sat down. "I may be slightly responsible for what happened."

"How could that be?" Brigid asked as she leaned forward. "Did you do this? Did you take down our website?"

"No, no," Vega said, shaking her head. "Let me explain. Sometimes I design programs and things like that. I had someone from school come to me and ask me to create a program so they could find a password. You know, a password that they could use to break into someone else's website. I'm pretty sure that's what was used to get into your website."

She looked extremely upset and as if she was about to break into tears. Brigid felt for the young girl. She could see that whatever it was Vega had done, she hadn't realized what the adverse consequences might be.

"What makes you think that?" Brigid asked, curious. How could this girl have become involved in this?

"It's like this. I wasn't sure I could trust this person, so I made a backdoor where I could check and see what he'd used it for," Vega explained. "It took me a little while to remember, because he bought it from me before all of this happened to you. Then, when I did remember, I had to check it out before I told you. I didn't want to risk getting in trouble for selling it if I didn't have to," Vega sighed.

Holly spoke up. "When Vega told me what had happened, I was determined to figure out who it was. Vega couldn't remember the guy's name, so I got my yearbook out and we started flipping through it."

"That was a good idea," Brigid nodded. "Did you find him?"

"We did," Vega said proudly. "I also have his IP address and matched it up. I know he's the one who hacked your website. I can get you back into your website if you'd like me to." She grinned, happy to make up for her mistake.

"No, I don't think I want to do it that way," Brigid said shaking her head. "I think it would be smarter to scare him. Why did he attack our website anyway?"

"Word has it that he doesn't like me for some reason," Holly shrugged. "I'm not really sure why, but that's what we've heard through other people." She looked at Vega who nodded.

"He's kind of a, um, jerk," Vega added. "You know, one of those guys who thinks he's awesome, but he isn't." She made a face like she smelled something bad. "He walks around like he owns the place and treats anyone he doesn't see as useful like crap."

Brigid nodded. "Okay. Why don't you tell me where he lives and any information you have on him? I have a plan."

"What are you going to do?" Holly asked.

"Make sure he learns a lesson," Brigid said with a smile. "But first, Vega, you know you shouldn't be doing that sort of thing. What if he had done something much worse with what you gave him? Legally, you could be charged as an accessory for whatever crime he might happen to commit."

Brigid didn't know how else to say it. Obviously, Vega was a smart girl. She didn't need to be making stupid choices that could land her in a lot of trouble.

"I won't," she said, shaking her head emphatically. "I've learned my lesson. That's for sure. I never thought something like this would happen. I mean, I know getting into something password protected probably isn't a smart thing to do, but I was thinking more along the lines of someone changing their grades or something like that. Not really good, but not the end of the world. I didn't think about someone using it to break into a website and causing damage to the owners. I probably should have, but I just didn't."

"And now you know that people can't always be trusted," Brigid said. "You don't want to assume the worst of everyone, but you also don't want to be too trusting of them and end up in a lot of trouble that wasn't really caused by you."

"I do," Vega said, nodding. "I sent the proof to Holly. She can forward it to you if you need it," Vega sighed. "I should have questioned why he wanted a password program, but I didn't automatically think it would be for a bad reason. I mean, yeah, I assumed he was getting into something he didn't have the password for, and it was pretty naïve of me not to think beyond that what the possible consequences might be."

"We all make mistakes," Brigid said gently. "It's what you do after them that shows your character. As long as you know that what you did was wrong and make sure you don't ever let it happen again, that's what matters. Learn from your mistakes and do what you can to clean up any damage that's been done along the way."

"Hey, Vega," Linc called out from the kitchen, "Would you like to stay for dinner?"

"I'd love to," she said with a grin. "It smells amazing."

"He's really a great cook," Holly explained. "Brigid is too, but what Linc does is out of this world." She grinned before standing up and heading over to see what he was cooking. "Looks like a pork roast," she said as she peered over the edge of the pot.

"That's because it is," Linc said with a grin. "And I particularly think you'll like the lemon buttermilk cake."

"I have to call Sheriff Davis," Brigid said as she stood up and reached for her phone. "He's going to want to know what we found out, and I need his help for the plan I've come up with."

CHAPTER SEVENTEEN

Brigid took her phone with her to her office and shut the door. She'd taken the piece of paper with the boy's information on it and saw that his name was Gage Morton. The name didn't ring any bells, but that didn't mean the sheriff wouldn't know who he or his parents were. After all, Cottonwood Springs was a small town.

Brigid felt like she was on an emotional rollercoaster. When she got home, she'd felt depressed and helpless. Now, thanks to Holly's friend Vega, she felt like she was in control again. It was beginning to look like there was an end in sight to the B & B website issue, and she felt much better because of it.

She pressed in the sheriff's personal number and waited as she listened to it ring.

"Davis," he said by way of answering his phone.

"I think we've found out who took the website down," Brigid said as she jumped into the conversation. She knew the sheriff would recognize her voice as soon as she spoke.

"Oh? Already?" he said, clearly surprised. "Brigid, ya' gotta' teach me yer' ways."

"I have a good team," she said with a smile. "I wouldn't have been able to do half of what I've done if it wasn't for them."

"Okay, get me up to speed here. What did ya' find out?" he asked. Brigid explained everything from Vega and the password program to the boy having something against Holly and for some reason taking down the site. "Ya' got evidence of this?" he asked.

"I do," she said. "I'll send it over after we end the call. I was thinking that maybe just a conversation might be enough to take care of the situation," she said hopefully. If all of this was true, the boy was misguided. She didn't want something like this permanently on his record. Once they had their website back, and he handed over the program, there would be no harm done.

"I see what yer' saying," Sheriff Davis said. "And yer' probably right. I'll come get ya' and we'll go pay him a visit."

"Can it wait just a little bit?" Brigid asked. "Linc is just serving dinner, and it's one of my favorites."

"I don't think the boy will be goin' anywhere durin' yer' dinner. Yeah, I can do a little paperwork while yer' eatin'. Jes' text me when yer' done," he said.

"Will do," Brigid replied. She switched over to her email and found the document Holly had forwarded to her. On it Vega had neatly laid out what his IP address was, showed him going to the website, and the times he went there. It also showed a log that seemed to be what the program sent back to Vega. Brigid was very glad Vega had been smart enough to watch what he was doing after she delivered the program to him in the first place.

After she'd forwarded the email on to Sheriff Davis, Brigid happily returned to her family in the other room.

"I'm going to take a little trip with the sheriff after dinner," Brigid said as she walked into the room.

"Okay," Linc said. He put a plate in front of Holly and Vega before he returned to the kitchen for his and Brigid's plates. "I was thinking that the girls and I would go and grab some ice cream to go with the cake. This is the best mood I've been in since this whole thing started."

"There's nothing better than ice cream and cake," Holly said happily.

Brigid joined them at the table and smiled. She was so incredibly grateful for the help the two young girls had provided. Granted, Vega had a major part in this whole thing, but she'd played an unknowing part. Watching her laugh at one of Linc's jokes, Brigid just knew she was a good kid and hoped she'd learned her lesson. That was what was important.

Jett and Lucky could smell the food and came trotting over from wherever they'd been and happily sat at everyone's feet. They knew that Linc would sneak them something when he thought Brigid wasn't looking. She always saw him do it, but pretended as though she hadn't.

After dinner, Brigid sent the sheriff a text and said good bye to Linc, Holly, and Vega as they left to get the ice cream. Once they pulled away, she went to the bathroom to run a brush through her hair and make sure she hadn't gotten any food on her blouse. Just as she decided she was satisfied with how she looked, there was a knock at the front door.

"Coming!" she called as she hurried through the great room. She hadn't expected the sheriff to get there so fast. Her original plan was to make sure she was ready and then sit outside and get some fresh evening air before he showed up. She was a little disappointed, but getting their website up and running again was far more important.

She pulled the door open, and it took her a moment to realize it wasn't the sheriff standing at the door. She blinked and saw that it was Abra instead.

"Is this a bad time?" Abra asked. "I don't normally pop by

unannounced, but I almost couldn't help it."

"I'm waiting for the sheriff to pick me up," Brigid explained as she stepped out onto the porch. "But I can visit with you until he gets here."

Abra nodded and stepped back. They both moved over to the nearby metal and glass table with two cushioned chairs. "And just so you know, I'm not a crazy stalker. Your sister told me where you live," she said as she smiled nervously as she sat down.

"I kind of figured," Brigid said. "Otherwise I would have been a little worried."

"It's just," Abra began. "Ever since I met you in person at Fiona's, there's a message that has been lodged in my brain. I know you aren't really big on the whole psychic thing, and I try to always respect that, but this message is insistent. I'm afraid if I don't pass it on, it's going to drive me nuts."

"Oh?" Brigid asked, unsure of how to respond to what she said. "It's not that I don't believe in psychics," she began. "It's more of a wariness. I'm not quite as quick to believe as Fiona is."

"I get that," Abra said as she nodded. "I'm kind of the same way. I used to deny that I could have conversations with those who had passed, but it caused me so much anxiety and stress, that I finally had to embrace it. Now it's become a big part of my life. I just need to tell you what I feel compelled to pass on to you. You can totally dismiss it as hogwash if you want, but please, would you at least let me get it out of my head?"

Brigid had never thought about the other side of the psychic thing. How frustrating would it be if you actually received messages from spirits and you weren't able to pass the message along because the person didn't want to listen to you? That wasn't the type of thing Brigid felt comfortable saddling someone she barely knew with. Slowly she nodded and said, "Okay. I'm sorry, I never thought about it that way."

"Oh, please don't feel bad," Abra said quickly. "After all, I'm the one who has chosen to do this. But I really feel that the person wanting to pass this information on is being insistent. It's like they have to get this across to you. That's why I'm here without an appointment," she said in a slightly apologetic tone of voice.

"Alright, I'm listening," Brigid said.

"Okay, give me one moment to settle in," she said and she took a long deep breath. Closing her eyes, she rolled her head as if she was popping her neck, and then her shoulders dropped. "I get both of your parents, but it seems as though your mother wants to speak first," Abra began. She opened her eyes and looked at her hands. "She's telling me she went very quickly and that you weren't prepared."

"Yes, that's true," Brigid said with a nod. She was listening to Abra, but so far, she wasn't convinced her mother had told Abra that. She felt that Fiona could have told Abra.

"She's showing me roses, and I can smell them too. Did she like them?" she asked.

"She did," Brigid said. "It was one of her favorite scents."

"Okay, good," Abra continued. "I'm now getting the feeling that there were harsh words said, like there was a phone call that was abrupt." She looked up into Brigid's eyes. "Your mother called you a couple of days before she died. You two disagreed over something. I feel like it's a husband, but not who you're married to now."

"No, it's not. I was married before," Brigid said but her words came out choked. No one knew about her mother calling her days before, not even Fiona.

"Okay, thank you for that. It was kind of throwing me off, but now I can see how that fits. Alright. She was telling you this guy wasn't right for you, wasn't she? She told you basically that she didn't like the guy and that you needed to find your true love."

Abra's words cut Brigid deeply. Everything she was saying was true. But there were only three people who knew about that disagreement and that was her mom, dad and Brigid. There was absolutely no way Abra could have known about this from anyone else, not even Fiona.

"She was doing this because on some level her soul knew that her time here on earth was short. Of course she didn't consciously know, but somewhere deep down, she did. In that conversation, she was telling you everything she'd wanted to tell you for a long time," Abra explained.

When she heard that, Brigid felt as though her throat had been closed off. She had to force herself to take a slow and steady breath. It was as if her world was tipping, and she was almost afraid to breathe for fear of upsetting the balance.

"She says you didn't accept the information as well as she would have liked," Abra continued. "You didn't want to hear it, is what she's saying."

"I didn't," Brigid admitted. "I think it was more out of fear that what she was saying was right. I knew my husband and I weren't right together, but I was trying to stick with my marriage."

"She understood, and she wasn't mad at you for that. If anything, she was proud. She knew she'd raised you to not just cut and run, that you would try to make things work, even when things were against you. She was a little frustrated with that trait at the time, but she had to respect it too, if that makes sense?" Abra seemed to be struggling to express herself.

"It does," Brigid nodded. "I get what you're trying to say."

"She wants you to dismiss it from your mind and not let it bother you anymore. She said you've already punished yourself enough. Let it go. You were doing what you thought was right in the moment and that's that." Abra smiled a little and Brigid could almost hear her mother's voice.

"She always said those words," Brigid smiled. "And that's that."

Abra chuckled. "They have a way of getting me to say words just the way they would. I think it's to help you know it's really them."

"I'm getting chills and feel like I could tear up," Brigid admitted as she rubbed her arms.

"It's all okay," Abra said softly. "That's the main message from your mother. Your dad is now stepping forward," she said as she started to stare at the side of the house. It was almost as if she had to focus on something farther away so she could concentrate. "He says he's sorry."

"What on earth for?" Brigid asked, surprised.

"That you and your sister had to deal with everything after he passed. He didn't want it to be like that, but it was simply the way it was supposed to go. The entire process made you and your sister even closer, didn't it?" Abra asked.

"It did. We were close before but after, even when we didn't talk, we could pick up again like there had never been a gap," Brigid supplied.

"He regrets everything working out that way, but he loved your mother too much to be without her. It's beautiful really. They had a great connection," Abra said.

"They did," Brigid admitted. "And I was always upset in my first marriage because I didn't feel like we had what my parents had."

"And now?" Abra asked.

"And now I do." Brigid smiled as a single tear slipped down her cheek.

"Fabulous," Abra said with a clap. "Oh, I feel so much lighter. You don't understand!" She began fanning herself as she leaned back in the chair. "I might actually get a whole night's sleep!"

"I'm sorry about all of that," Brigid apologized.

"It's all good," Abra said. "Don't worry about it."

The sound of an approaching vehicle made them both look out at the driveway. They could see the word "Sheriff" written on the side of the black truck.

"Looks like he's here," Abra said. "I'll take off. Thank you for listening."

"No, thank you for making me listen," Brigid said as they both stood up. "You just took a lot of weight off of me, too."

"Good," said Abra with a satisfied smile.

CHAPTER EIGHTEEN

"You have company?" Sheriff Davis asked as Brigid climbed into the passenger seat of his truck.

"Yes, but she was ready to leave," Brigid explained. "She just dropped by really quick to tell me something."

He nodded and seemed like he was going to say more, but decided against it. Instead, he pulled out of the driveway and headed down the road. "Okay, lemme get this straight. We're going to go in there and scare this kid straight, right? But then we're only going to give him a little slap on the wrist if he's remorseful," he surmised.

"That was what I had planned, unless you can think of something better?" she asked.

"No, I'm fine with it. But if this kid starts acting like a little punk, I'm gonna' at least give him some volunteer work to do," he warned.

"Hey, you do whatever feels right," Brigid said as she raised her hands in a sign of mock surrender. "You know where I stand. I think we've done this enough times now," she said with a smirk.

He nodded curtly at her before reaching for a piece of gum. Unwrapping it, he shoved it in his mouth before speaking again. "I kinda' know Gage Morton's dad. We was in the same grade in school.

Both of us were local kids, ya' know? Remember Bobby Morton from your school days here in Cottonwood Springs?"

"Vaguely," Brigid said. "But you're younger than I am. I'm sure Fiona probably knows him."

He nodded. "Yeah, bet she does. Anyway, his dad ain't gonna' be too pleased with him. Even if we don't do anythin' to him, ya' can bet yer' bottom dollar his dad will. But that's on him," he said with a slight shrug.

A few minutes later they pulled up in front of a tan colored house whose yard was starting to get shaggy. The house itself was L shaped with a long screened-in porch along the front of it.

"I'm purty sure that's Bobby's truck in the garage," Sheriff Davis commented. "So at least he'll be here for this."

Brigid nodded and stopped in front of the screen door to the porch as the sheriff held it open for her. She stepped up on the porch, her footsteps sounding loud on the wood. Sheriff Davis stepped around her and knocked on the door. It was the kind of knock that could be heard through an entire house.

It didn't take long before a balding, heavy-set man opened the door. He had a goatee with the faintest hint of grey in it. "Well, Sheriff, having you knock on my door is certainly a surprise," he said when he saw who it was. "What can I do for you?"

"Unfortunately, I need to talk to ya' 'bout your son, Gage," Sheriff Davis said as he opened his jacket and pulled out some papers. Brigid saw they were printouts of what she'd emailed him. "He seems to have made a poor choice recently."

"Well, come on in and sit a spell. We'll see what my boy's gotten into now," Bobby said as he pulled the door open farther for them to step inside the house.

"Thank ya'," Sheriff Davis said. "This is Brigid Olsen. She's a consultant of mine," he explained.

Bobby shook her hand with a nice firm grip. "Nice to meet you, Brigid. I've been hearing about all the good things you've been doing around here."

"Thank you," she said with a smile. "Always happy to help."

"Gage," Bobby yelled as he turned towards a narrow hallway. "Get your butt out here, boy."

Bobby motioned for them to sit down on the couch and turned down the TV. The front room was small and a little cramped, but comfortable. The couch was older with a crocheted afghan on the back. Family photos lined the wall above it.

"What?" said a young man with red hair who emerged from the hallway, looking confused. He was tall and thickly built, like his father.

"The sheriff says you've been getting into something you shouldn't have been in," Bobby said with a deep voice. "Get over here while I hear what you've been doing."

Gage looked nervous as he walked towards the chair next to his father. He started picking at his fingernails as he sat down.

"Got a coupla' papers here that trace your son's online, uh, trail, I guess would be the word," Sheriff Davis began to explain. "He purchased a computer program from a girl at school that would help him get into things that are password protected. He got into the website of the New Dawn B & B that Brigid and her husband Linc will be openin' soon and took the entire thing down, essentially shuttin' down their B & B right before the grand openin'."

Laying it all out like that, Brigid thought it sounded much worse than what she'd initially thought. But Sheriff Davis was right. This boy had taken it upon himself to shut down a business right before its grand opening and for what reason? Jealousy? Anger? Whatever his reasoning, it was petty and could potentially cost Linc and Brigid a lot of money.

"Is this true?" Bobby asked as he turned toward his son. "Did you do this?"

"Well, I-. I mean, I just-," Gage stammered.

"It's a simple yes or no question, Gage. Did ya' take down their website?" Sheriff Davis asked.

Gage opened his mouth as if he was going to say something else but then shut it. Looking defeated he muttered, "Yes."

"Why would you do something stupid like that?" Bobby asked. "What reason could you possibly have for shutting down someone's business?" Bobby seemed almost hurt by the fact that his son had done it.

"I wasn't doing it because of their business," Gage said quickly. "Honestly, I didn't even really think about it that way. It was just Holly-," he said, but his father cut him off.

"Holly? Who is she and what does she have to do with it?" Bobby asked.

"She's my daughter," Brigid interjected. "She's the one who built the website for us."

"Yeah, and everyone was making a big deal about it. Everyone's always talking about how great she is. I just wanted to shut everyone up. I didn't want to see one more example of how she was better than me," Gage grumbled.

"Gage, that's a terrible excuse for almost ruining a business," Bobby said. He was clearly frustrated with his son for his actions.

"I know, I'm sorry," Gage said looking down at the floor.

Bobby gave his son a long look before turning back to the sheriff and Brigid. "Tell me what I can do. How can we make this right? Whatever it is, you name it."

"First things first. I want their website restored," Sheriff Davis said matter of factly. "Like right now. They've had this grand openin' planned fer quite awhile, and I'd hate to see it have to be postponed 'cause of this."

"Understandable," Bobby said with a nod. "Gage, go get your laptop and fix their website."

"Dad, I-," Gage began but his father cut him off.

"I don't want to hear any excuses. Just do it," he said forcefully.

"I also want the program he used," Sheriff Davis said.

"Of course," Bobby said. "Bring that program and your laptop out here, pronto." Gage stood up and hurried back down the hall. "I'm so sorry, Brigid. I had no idea he even knew how to do something like this. Please extend my apologies to your husband and daughter. I'm not sure what got into him, but believe me, his mother and I raised Gage better than this."

"I understand," Brigid said softly. "You can't watch them all the time, can you?"

"No, ma'am you can't. I thought I had a fairly good eye on him, but I guess I was wrong," he sighed.

"Hey, don't beat yerself up," Sheriff Davis said. "Kids are gonna' get in trouble once in a while. Jes' natural. At least in this situation, everythin' can be put right again."

"That's true," Bobby said as Gage returned. "I just never expected my son to do something so foolish."

"You did raise me better, Dad," Gage grumbled. "I was just mad."

"Mad at what? What could this girl have possibly done to you for you to take down her parent's business so you could get back at her?" Bobby insisted.

Brigid was curious too. Had Holly been doing something she wasn't aware of?

"She didn't do anything," Gage said. "It's just, everyone's always talking about how smart she is and all the great things she does. It's like she's some sort of celebrity or something. Everyone seems to love her." He pushed open his laptop and started typing.

"That's no excuse," Bobby said shaking his head. "You can't be jealous because she's getting attention and think it justifies your behavior."

"It's not like Holly hasn't struggled too," Brigid chimed in. "She's had a tough life getting to where she is now. I'm sure you remember that her mother was murdered and that was just the tip of the iceberg of what she's lived through.

"She's smart because she used her education as a way of coping with all the negativity in her life. Instead of focusing on everything that was going wrong in her life, she opened a book and took her mind off of all of it. She just happened to have a great memory and retained most of it. But I'm sure there are things you can do that she can't."

"Yeah? Like what?" Gage grumbled.

"For one, she can't play football. She's not the greatest at catching, that's for sure," Brigid chuckled. "I think it also took someone pretty smart to take down that website. Don't be so hard on yourself. Your strengths are just different than hers. I believe some teachers remember her struggles and tend to point her out because she's done so well."

"I guess so," Gage mumbled. "Okay, your website's all back up like it was," he sighed. He turned his laptop around and showed everyone it was online. Brigid couldn't believe how relieved she felt when she saw it back online again.

"Thank you," she said.

"Now, I'd like to have that program, and ya' need to remove it from yer' computer," Sheriff Davis began.

"I think maybe you should just take the laptop, too," Bobby said. "Have someone else make sure it's removed completely. Gage is smart, and I don't want him to try to pull something."

"I'm not going to pull anything," Gage grumbled.

"Still, hand it all over to the sheriff," Bobby insisted. He watched as his son closed the laptop and passed everything over. He turned to the sheriff and said, "Take your time with it, too. He won't be needing it for a while."

"But how am I supposed to do my homework?" Gage whined.

"You can do it on the family computer," Bobby said firmly. "You gave up your privilege of having a laptop when you started doing things you shouldn't have been doing. That's the price you pay for making a bad choice."

Brigid tried not to smile. It was nice to see a parent who was fully invested in making sure his son learned a lesson. She'd been afraid that the whole situation might be dismissed by his parents. At least now she knew there was a lesson being learned from it.

"And don't worry, there's gonna' be repercussions for the person who provided the program as well. But I think it's best for everybody involved that this issue not get discussed with the general public," Sheriff Davis said. "I know fer a fact that Coach Thomas wouldn't look too kindly on havin' one of his football players gettin' in trouble." He raised his eyebrow at Gage to make sure what he was hinting at hit home.

Gage swallowed hard. "He'd bench me for sure," he said. "I can't be benched. It's my senior year."

"Which is why I'm tryin' to go easy on ya'," Sheriff Davis said. "But don't forget that what ya' did was a crime. This could have gone very differently if it wasn't fer Mrs. Olsen here. She jes' wanted her site back, no harm and no foul. But had she decided to press charges….," he let his sentence trail off. 'Well, I think ya' know that wouldn't have been a good thing fer ya'."

"I get it, and I'm sorry," Gage said. "I truly am. I'll try to make it up to you."

"Maybe you can mow their yard all summer for them for free," Bobby offered. "That could be a start."

Gage didn't look too pleased, but he nodded. "I could," he admitted.

"We can talk about it later," Brigid said. "But for now, just do good in school, okay?"

Gage nodded.

"We'll leave ya' be," Sheriff Davis said. "Thank ya' so much fer yer' cooperation." He and Brigid stood up and started walking towards the door, Bobby following them.

"Anytime," Bobby said. "Once again, I'm sorry for the trouble he put you through." They all shook hands and Sheriff Davis and Brigid headed back to his truck.

"I think that went well," Sheriff Davis said with a grin.

"I think you're right," Brigid said. "And the bonus is that now Linc won't have to mow the lawn this summer," she said with a smile.

CHAPTER NINETEEN

"I still can't believe it was Gage Morton," Holly said as she shook her head. It was several days later and everyone was sitting around Holly's laptop, waiting for the clock to count down to zero and their reservations would be open. There was a fairly large group that had collected in the house including Linc, Brigid, and Holly. Wade had joined them, along with Vega, Levi, Fiona, and little Aiden.

"I can," Wade muttered. "The guy hasn't been the most upstanding citizen, that's all I'm saying."

"He wouldn't have been able to do it if it hadn't been for me," Vega sighed.

"Oh, he probably still would have tried," Brigid pointed out.

"He looks at me like I'm some sort of alien or something," Levi sighed.

"Think it could be the periwinkle hair you've been sporting recently?" Holly suggested with a smirk.

"Hey, my hair looks amazing," Levi said defensively as he gently touched it. Everyone couldn't help but laugh.

"It's getting closer," Holly said as she looked at the timer.

"Oh my gosh, I can't believe how nervous I am," Linc said from where he was leaning over the couch. "It's almost like a New Year's celebration or something. You know, waiting for the ball to drop."

Brigid knew exactly what he meant. There was an excited, anticipatory feeling in the air. "Remember, just because it goes live, that doesn't mean you're going to instantly get reservations," she warned Linc. "That's not what this is about."

"No, I know," Linc nodded. "Everyone's here to eat and celebrate our new beginning with us," he said with a grin. "And I really am glad you guys are all here."

"When you said lasagna, that was all it took for me," Wade admitted. "Just smelling that and your garlic bread is making my stomach growl."

"It's almost done," Linc promised. "Oh look, ten more seconds!"

Brigid started counting down out loud and everyone else joined in. Holly had the counter in a smaller window above the one that showed their website. That way, when it went to zero, all she had to do was refresh the page.

"Zero!" they all said and Holly clicked the refresh button. Now there was a reservation button and all the forms were up and waiting for guests to start filling them out.

"And now we wait," Linc said as he turned towards the kitchen. "Who else is ready to eat?"

"Me!" a handful of voices said together and they all began to migrate over to the dining room table. Brigid and Holly helped Linc serve their guests as they all found seats at the large table. One by one, they dished out a serving on each plate and then Holly walked the plate over to each of the guests.

"This is almost what it would be like over at the B & B if we had a bunch of guests," Linc observed.

"Only we'd be serving breakfast rather than dinner," she pointed out. "But I do think your praline apple French toast casserole would be good for the first breakfast at the B & B."

"Still, it feels great," Linc smiled. "Having everyone here, enjoying each other's company. Even if we don't get a single reservation for a couple of days, I'm happy."

"Good," Brigid said as she gave him a kiss. "I am too."

When everyone had been served, the three of them got their plates and joined the others at the table. At first the conversation was scattered, but then it turned into a full table discussion.

"I've started working on your websites, Fiona," Holly said. "And Levi agreed to take some photos for me to add this weekend."

"Tell me," Levi said as he leaned closer to Fiona. "Do you make clothes for guys, too?"

"I hadn't really thought about it," Fiona said as she blinked. "But I guess I could."

"Man, that would be awesome. I really like the simplicity of what you do, while still making it all look so nice. Like a comfortable fancy, you know?"

Fiona tossed her head back and laughed. "You know, I hadn't thought about it that way, but you're right. That is kind of what I shoot for. Something nice enough to wear almost anywhere, but comfortable enough you don't want to change out of it."

"See, that's what I'm talking about," Levi said. "Those are the clothes people want. I'm telling you, you're going to turn some heads. You just need the right social media presence. Get a couple of profiles with some great pictures of your clothes and a beautiful model or two to wear them." He gave a pointed look at Brigid and Holly when he said the words, "beautiful model."

"Oh, I don't think I should be modeling anything," Brigid said bashfully. "Holly looks amazing in whatever she wears, but I'm not so sure I'd do the clothes justice."

"Puhlleeze," Levi said waving her concerns away. "If I take your picture, you'll look just as stunning as you do every day."

"I would like to show that my clothes aren't just for teens," Fiona said as she looked at her sister hopefully. "Maybe if I make some stuff for men, we can get Linc in on it too."

"You know it!" Linc said joyfully. "I'd rock that catwalk like you wouldn't believe." He grinned, which made Brigid shake her head.

"See, Linc's in on it. That means you have to, Brigid," Fiona said with a smirk before taking another bite.

"You guys are terrible, you know that?" Brigid laughed. "This feels like peer pressure. I think I'm a little old for peer pressure."

"You're not old. I wish you'd stop saying that," Holly grumbled.

"I think you're beautiful and would do a great job," Vega said softly.

"Heck yeah she would," Wade said, joining in. "I'd help pass the word around, too. I have quite a few friends on social media. I'm sure a few of them would also pass it on."

"Then it's settled," Fiona said. "You guys will be my models. Now I just have to figure out how to market on social media."

"I can help," Levi said. "I actually took some classes online and got certified as a social media specialist."

"Are you serious?" Holly asked.

"Yeah, why?" Levi asked, surprised.

"There are tons of things you can do online now," Vega said. "A lot of these tech jobs don't require a lot of education, just knowledge. You'd be surprised."

"So, Levi," Brigid began. "What are you thinking of doing career wise?"

"I'm not sure," he shrugged. "I don't really feel like I have much to work with."

"Are you kidding?" Wade said with a mouth full of lasagna. He quickly chewed and swallowed. "You should be a photographer. You do a great job, and I'm sure you could get lots of business once you get going."

"You think?" Levi asked surprised. "I mean, I love doing it. That's for sure. But I never really considered trying to do that as my profession."

"There are lots of ways you could make money," Fiona interjected. "You could go online and sell prints of any general pictures you take right now. I know a lady online who does that. They have places where you can get your pictures and print them on coffee mugs or calendars or whatever."

"Wow, I didn't know that," Levi admitted. "I guess I wasn't looking at the big picture."

"And what about you, Wade? What are your plans?" Linc asked as they continued to eat.

"I've just about decided I'm going to go to college to become a lawyer," he said with a smile.

"Really?" Brigid asked. "That's wonderful."

"My parents are a little stressed, because they don't exactly make a ton of money. But I've started looking into scholarships that I could get, and I'm hoping to get recruited somewhere to play baseball," he said. "That's the one thing I'm really crossing my fingers for. I know I still have time, but it's important to stand out early when it comes to sports."

"I'd think so," Brigid said. "There are a lot of kids out there competing for those sports scholarships."

Wade nodded. "There are, but I'm just going to do my best and see where it takes me."

"That's all you can do," Linc said. "Sometimes that's the only thing you can do. Just plan and see what comes up."

"And you, Vega?" Brigid asked.

"I want to be a software engineer," Vega said. "I don't know if I'll go to college or not at this point. I've been working on building a portfolio online to showcase my work. If I'm lucky, I'm hoping I'll be approached by some big company and get to jump right in."

"I'll be rooting for you," Brigid said with a smile. "You seem to really know your stuff."

There was a ding nearby that made everyone look around. "What was that?" Linc finally asked. He began feeling in his pockets for his phone. "Was that my phone?"

"I think so," Brigid said as she turned in her chair. "Your phone's over on the counter, and it's lit up."

"Oh my gosh," Holly said. She'd pulled her phone out, too. "You just got your first reservation!"

"What?" Linc asked as he pushed his chair back and walked over to retrieve his phone.

"I put an app on your phone and mine that sends a notification whenever you get a reservation. Look," Holly said as she held up her phone. She directed it towards Brigid first and then around the table.

"They booked for a few days from now!"

"She's right," Linc said as he stood near the counter and looked at his phone. "It's right here. They booked for a two-night stay in the Blue Room." His voice was distant as if he couldn't believe it.

"Congratulations guys!" Fiona cheered. "Your first reservation!"

Brigid stood up from the table and went to look over Linc's shoulder. He was scrolling through the information, reading it along with him. "You did it," she said softly in his ear. There was a feeling of pride swelling up in her. She was so proud of this man she married.

Not only had he taken a huge risk, but he'd followed his heart, and it looked like it had been the right thing to do. Someone out there had been on their list and ready to reserve. That really meant something.

"No, babe. We did it," he said as he turned towards her. "We are now officially open for business and actually have a guest coming in a few days. If you hadn't believed in me and kept me focused on what was important, I don't know if we would have gotten this far." He wrapped his arms around her waist and pulled her close.

"Of course we would have," she said with a grin. "It just might have taken a little longer. I'm pretty sure you would have still been rearranging furniture if I hadn't finally put my foot down." She wrapped her arms around his neck and ran her fingers through his hair.

"That's probably true," he chuckled. "And none of this would have been possible without Holly and Levi making our website look so amazing and inviting." Linc gave Brigid a quick kiss before turning towards everyone at the table.

"And thanks to the rest of you for either helping get us back up and running or simply just listening to us and dealing with our crankiness. I know we were all ready for this day to finally come."

"I'm really proud of you guys," Fiona said with a smile. "The New Dawn B & B is off to a great start."

They heard the same chime again, and everyone turned towards Linc. He, instead, looked at Holly. "Why would it make another sound?" he asked.

"I'm not sure," she said as she pulled out her phone. "It shouldn't do reminder notifications or anything."

"No, look," Brigid said as she took Linc's phone from him. "You got another reservation for a couple of days after the other one. This one is for Holly's room. It says in the notes that they'll be on their honeymoon."

"Two reservations already?" Fiona grinned. "You guys better get ready. I think you're going to be busier than you ever thought you would."

Linc grinned and looked at Brigid. "Are you ready for your guests, Mrs. Olsen?"

"As long as I have you," she said. "I'm ready for anything."

EPILOGUE

"Oh my gosh, they're here," Holly said as she hurried away from the window. It was the day that their first guest was expected to arrive, and all three of them were nervous and anxious waiting for them to show up. Ever since they'd gotten up that morning, they'd been over at the B & B, cleaning and making sure the place was in tip-top shape for their very first guest.

Linc took his place near the registration desk while Brigid adjusted the pillows on the couch. Holly bolted for the kitchen, disappearing from sight.

Brigid saw the couple approach the door through the window and had to force herself to remain calm. Part of her wanted to run over and jerk the door open for them and take their bags too. But she knew that would seem extremely odd and probably make them want to run in the other direction. So instead, she forced herself to stay put.

The door opened and she watched a smile spread across Linc's face. "Hello," he said brightly. "Welcome to the New Dawn B & B. Do you need any help with your bags?"

"No thank you," the man said as he shut the door behind them. "We've got them covered."

Brigid watched as Linc checked them in. They were slightly older than Brigid and Linc, but not by much. The woman was short with curly brown hair and a gentle smile. The man was almost a foot taller than her with mostly gray hair. Both of them were extremely polite.

"We couldn't wait until we were able to book with you," the man said. "We love to visit B & B's and make it a habit to visit all the ones that jump out at us. Even if it's just for a night. Gives us a reason to get away."

"That's wonderful," Linc said happily. "I'm glad you decided to come and stay with us. We'll do our very best to live up to your expectations. We're still working out the kinks and such, so if you have any feedback for us, please don't hesitate to let my wife, Brigid, and me know." He gestured towards Brigid, and she drew closer to introduce herself.

"I just love getting to meet new people when we stay somewhere," the wife said. "It's so much more personal than staying at a hotel. At a B & B, you get to know real people and enjoy real company."

"That's exactly why we decided to open one," Brigid admitted. "We had such a wonderful experience in San Antonio at one that it left a very real impression on us. Then, a friend suggested we open one and we thought, why not?" She chuckled and Linc nodded.

"Well you've done a wonderful job on it," the husband said. "It's a beautiful place. Not too frilly, but not too manly. A nice balance of both worlds."

"Thank you," Linc said. "Let me show you to your room, then you can get comfortable and relax."

Linc led them down the hallway to their room, and Holly emerged from the kitchen.

"Well, they seem nice," she said as she looked after them.

"They do," Brigid nodded.

"I guess Gage Morton got in some serious trouble from his dad," Holly began. She followed Brigid to the kitchen where she started checking the cabinets to make sure they had everything for the next couple of days.

"Oh?" Brigid asked. "How do you know that?"

"Wade said he heard it from someone who's on the football team. I guess his dad pretty much took everything away. He even sits in the stands during Gage's football practices. Of course, there's no games going on since it's not that time of year. But still, they have practice to stay in shape and stuff. His dad brings a book and hangs out, then drives Gage home." Holly shook her head as if that was the worst thing in the world.

"Is that so bad? Having your dad at practice?" Brigid asked with a raised eyebrow.

"I wouldn't think so, but I'm not trying to be some big bad football player. I think it probably puts a damper on him trying to look tough when his dad's driving him home from practice," Holly pointed out.

"Well, that's what happens when you do something stupid like hack into a business's website and take it down," Brigid pointed out. "I think the sheriff finally returned Gage's laptop to his parents. He said he was going to call them."

"I'm just glad Vega was able to help us out," Holly sighed. She grabbed an apple from the bowl on the counter and took a big bite out of it. "I'm not sure we would have ever figured it out if it hadn't been for her."

"You know, Holly, those are for the guests," Brigid said pointedly as she looked at the fruit bowl. "And you're right, I was at my wits end. I didn't want you to have to start all over again. Especially when we didn't know who took it down in the first place or why. After all, what if they would have just taken the new one as well?"

"Exactly," Holly said. "But in the end, it all worked out. And Vega is holding to her word. She's not selling anything to anyone. No more hackery type of stuff out of her."

"Hackery?" Brigid asked. "Is that even a word?"

Holly shrugged and took another big bite of her apple. "It is now, I just made it one. Feel free to use it in your day-to-day language. Just be sure to give the credit for it to me," she said with a wink.

"I don't know what I'm going to do with you, you know that?" Brigid said with a laugh.

"Eh, enjoy my company and sharp-witted humor, most likely," Holly said.

"That's for sure," Brigid said. "Have you given any more thought to what that Jack guy said?"

"Oh, yeah," Holly nodded. "He told me he really liked what I was doing with Fiona's websites. He gave me a few suggestions and even sent me a few links for places I could always learn more, if I was interested. I guess there are sites that teach you to code and stuff for free."

"Make sure you toss that apple core in the compost bin," Brigid said pointedly as she moved to the fridge to take inventory. She wanted to make sure there were plenty of eggs and milk as well as juice and fresh fruit. "So is that what you're going to do? Build websites?"

"I'm not really sure, to be honest," Holly admitted. "I mean, I like doing it, and it's fun. But I'm not sure it's nothing more than just a hobby."

"A hobby that apparently pays good money," Brigid said. "I heard the other day how much Fiona was offering you."

"I told her she didn't need to pay me," Holly said as she shook her head. "But she won't listen to me. She started saying something about an exchange of energy and wanting to keep the balance. I just went along with it. After all, if she really wants to give me money, I'm not going to turn it down."

"I understand where she's coming from. You put a lot of work into those websites. She doesn't want you using up your free time and not get anything out of it," Brigid pointed out.

"Yeah, but she's already making me all those clothes and stuff," Holly said. "I feel bad."

"Don't. She loves you and wants to do this for you. It means a lot to her. Just enjoy and remember to say thank you," Brigid said with a smile.

Linc entered the kitchen and clapped his hands. "Our first guests are settling into their room. They really liked it and said it was even nicer than they'd expected. Their exact words were, 'this room looked so nice in the pictures, but seeing it in person, it's even nicer than we anticipated.' I thought my heart would just burst with happiness," Linc said, grinning.

"Good," Brigid said with a nod.

"Did you hear that?" Linc asked as he turned around. "I think I just heard someone pull up."

"I'm not expecting anyone," Brigid said as they all went to the front room to look out the window. Once there, they saw a familiar face approaching the front door.

"It's Rich Jennings," Linc said happily. He went to the door and opened it for him. "Come on in, Rich. What brings you our way today?" he asked.

"I just thought I'd drop by. I heard from Corey that you were going to get your first guests today. I wanted to tell you congratulations." He looked around and smiled. "You've got a really nice place here. I looked over the photos online, but I always like to see a place in person. Gives me a better perspective."

"That it does," Linc said. "Our first guests arrived not long before you. They're in their room getting settled."

"Wonderful," Rich said. "I'm so glad you guys are doing this. It might be old fashioned of me, but I feel like it's good work. Like we're bringing people back together again. No more of this sterilized, corporate stuff. We're connecting with real people and spreading kindness as much as possible."

"I have to head out. I've got to work at the bookstore," Holly said as she gave hugs to Brigid and Linc. "I'll see you later Mr. Jennings," she said with a wave.

"You've got a good one there," Rich said. "I sure wish I could find the right woman and have a family, but I'm starting to think it's just not in the cards for me."

"You never know, Rich," Linc said supportively. "Look at us. I didn't think I'd ever have a kid and then what happened? We all came together to create a family."

"That's right," Brigid said with a nod. "We're like puzzle pieces that never fit anywhere else correctly."

"Maybe you're right," Rich sighed. "I guess I'll just have to keep my fingers crossed. Anyway, I'll get out of your hair, I don't want to bother you."

"You're no bother," Linc insisted. "Would you like to see the other rooms? I can give you the tour."

"That would be great, thank you," Rich said with a smile.

Linc led him along to the hallway while Brigid hung back. She'd watched Linc give the tour often enough that she knew exactly what he was going to say. She didn't need to hear it all over again. Instead, she headed for the office they kept in the B & B and searched for the list she'd compiled of the local B & B's that wanted to work with each other. There were only a couple that weren't interested, but she thought they might come around eventually.

She sat down at her computer and clicked on the icon where they could all come together and chat online. It was where they would reach out to one another and communicate. After all, you never know when you might need to put the word out about something. Brigid smiled to herself, knowing that this was the start of something good.

She looked at her personal messages and saw one from Nora Russo, the woman who owned the B & B over in New Haven. She and Brigid had started conversing off and on recently and had really hit it off. Brigid liked the woman's no-nonsense personality, while still being a kind person. It was refreshing, to say the least.

Nora had sent her a message saying that her bookings had increased since she'd made a few of the changes Holly had passed along. Holly was still supposed to make a new website for the woman, but she and a couple of friends had looked over the woman's online presence and made a few suggestions that Nora could implement until then.

She said she didn't know if it was the changes or what, but she was excited and glad that Brigid and Sheriff Davis had come knocking on her door that day. She hoped it was the beginning of something good for both of them.

Brigid smiled. It was always a great feeling when people stopped competing with each other and instead worked together. That was how real change happened.

I wonder if she's ever met Rich Jennings, she thought with a slight smile on her face.

RECIPES

LEMON BUTTERMILK CAKE

Ingredients:
Cake:
2 cups all-purpose flour
1 tsp. sea salt
1 tsp. baking powder
½ tsp. baking soda
2 cups sugar
2/3 cup buttermilk
½ cup vegetable oil
Finely grated zest from 2 lemons
6 tbsp. fresh lemon juice
1 tsp. vanilla extract
4 large eggs
Nonstick cooking spray

Syrup and Glaze:
1 ¼ cups plus 2 tbsp. powdered sugar, sifted
3 tbsp. plus 2 tsp. fresh lemon juice
2 tbsp. unsalted butter, melted
1 tbsp. whole milk

Directions:
Preheat oven to 350 degrees. Oil a 9" x 13" baking dish with

cooking spray.

In a large bowl, whisk together the flour, salt, baking powder, and baking soda. In a medium bowl, whisk together the sugar, oil, buttermilk, lemon zest, lemon juice, vanilla, and eggs until smooth. Pour the liquid ingredients over the dry ingredients until just combined. Pour the batter into the prepared pan and smooth out on top. Bake approximately 35 – 40 minutes, or until a toothpick inserted into the center of the cake comes out clean.

While the cake is baking, first make the syrup and then the glaze. In a small bowl, whisk together ¼ cup powdered sugar and 3 tbsp. lemon juice until they form a thin syrup. In another small bowl, whisk together the remaining one cup plus two tbsp. powdered sugar and 2 tsp. lemon juice, butter, and milk until they form a smooth glaze.

Remove the cake from the oven and let cool for 5 minutes. Using the tines of a fork, prick the top of the cake all over, making small holes to hold some of the syrup. Slowly drizzle the syrup evenly over the cake and let cake cool completely, about 45 minutes. Using a spoon, spread the glaze over the top of the cake. Serve and enjoy!

PRALINE APPLE FRENCH TOAST

Ingredients:
¾ cup unsalted butter, melted
¾ cup granulated sugar, divided
2/3 cup firmly packed brown sugar
2 cups pecan halves
6 cups high-quality white bread, torn into bite-size pieces
3 Golden Delicious apples, peeled, cored, and chopped into ½" pieces
6 large eggs
2 cups heavy cream
2 tsp. ground cinnamon
1 tbsp. vanilla extract

Nonstick cooking spray

Directions:
Coat a 9" x 13" baking dish with cooking spray. Combine the melted butter and both sugars in a medium-size bowl. Pour into baking dish. Scatter pecans on top.

Put the bread and apples into a large bowl. In a medium-size bowl, beat together the eggs, cream, cinnamon, sugar, and vanilla. Pour over the bread and apples and mix well. Pour over the mixture in the baking dish and refrigerate overnight.

Preheat oven to 350 degrees. Take the baking dish out of the refrigerator ½ hour prior to baking. Bake 45 – 55 minutes until puffed and golden brown. Let rest five minutes. Serve and enjoy!

PORK LOIN ROAST WITH MUSTARD SAUCE

Ingredients:
Roast:
4 lb. rolled boneless pork loin roast
½ cup firmly packed brown sugar
2 tsp. freshly ground black pepper
1 ½ tsp. ground cinnamon
½ tsp. Chinese 5 spice powder
2 tbsp. olive oil
Plastic wrap

Mustard Sauce:
3 tbsp. unsalted butter
¼ cup finely chopped shallots (If I don't have them, I use scallions or a white onion.)
1 tsp. chopped fresh sage
1 tsp. chopped fresh thyme
2 tbsp. all-purpose flour
¼ cup Dijon mustard
2 tbsp. dry white wine

1 cup beef broth (I use Better Than Bouillon.)
1 ½ cups heavy cream
Salt and freshly ground pepper to taste

Place the roast on a large piece of plastic wrap. In a small bowl, combine the brown sugar, pepper, salt, cinnamon, and 5 spice powder. Rub this all over the roast and wrap lightly in plastic wrap. Refrigerate for at least 8 hours and up to 24 hours.

One hour before ready to cook, remove pork from refrigerator and discard the plastic wrap. Preheat oven to 325 degrees. Heat the oil in a large ovenproof skillet over medium-high heat and brown the roast on all sides, about 2-3 minutes per side. Transfer the skillet to the oven and roast for one hour.

Remove from oven and cover loosely with aluminum foil for 15 minutes. Carve the roast into thin slices, plate and serve with the mustard sauce. Enjoy!

Mustard Sauce:
In a medium-size saucepan melt the butter. Add the shallots, sage, thyme, and cook, stirring until the shallots are a little softened, about 3 minutes.

Stir in the flour, whisking until white bubbles form on the surface. Continue to whisk 2 more minutes. Increase the heat and gradually add the mustard, wine, and broth, continuing to stir until the mixture comes to a boil.

Reduce the heat to low, stir in the cream, and continue stirring until the sauce is heated through and is smooth and thickened, about 10 minutes. Serve warm with the pork. Enjoy!

WHITE CHOCOLATE MACADAMIA NUT MUFFINS

Ingredients:
1 ¾ cups all-purpose flour

¾ cup sugar
2 ½ tsp. baking powder
½ tsp. salt
1 egg
½ cup milk
¼ cup unsalted butter, melted
¾ cup white chocolate baking chips
¾ cup macadamia nuts, chopped
Muffin pan
12 muffin liners

Glaze:
½ cup white baking chips
2 tbsp. heavy whipping cream

Directions:
Preheat oven to 400 degrees. In a large bowl combine flour, sugar, baking powder, and salt. In another bowl combine egg, milk, and butter. Stir into dry ingredients until moistened. Add chips and nuts.

Place muffin liners in muffin cups and fill 2/3 full. Bake 15 – 18 minutes or until a toothpick inserted into the center comes out clean. Cool on wire baking rack.

In a microwave, melt the chips with the cream. Stir until smooth. Drizzle over warm muffins. Serve and enjoy!

LIA'S APPLE PIE

Ingredients:
6 apples
½ cup raisins
¾ cup sugar
¾ tsp. ground cinnamon
1 prepared pie crust
4 tsp. lemon juice, divided

Directions:
Preheat the oven to 375 degrees. Pare, core, and chop the apples into ½" pieces. Put them into a large bowl with 2 tsp. lemon juice to keep them from becoming brown.

Put the remaining 2 tsp. lemon juice in a small bowl and put the raisins in the bowl. Mix well. Combine the sugar and cinnamon and set aside.

When ready to bake the pie, drain the apples and the raisins. When drained, place them in a bowl and mix in the sugar mixture. Spoon into the prepared pie crust and bake in oven for 20-25 minutes. Ovens vary so it may need a little more time. Let cool for five minutes. Serve and enjoy!

NOTE: This recipe came from a reader of mine, Lia Storm. She makes big batches of the apple pie mixture and freezes it. When she's ready to make a pie, she half-thaws the amount she wants to use in the pie, puts it in the oven and bakes it. Pretty nice to have on hand!

LEAVE A REVIEW

I'd really appreciate it you could take a few seconds and leave a review of Missing in the Islands.

Just go to the link below. Thank you so much, it means a lot to me ~ Dianne - http://getbook.at/MITI

Paperbacks & Ebooks for FREE

Go to www.dianneharman.com/freepaperback.html and get your FREE copies of Dianne's books and favorite recipes immediately by signing up for her newsletter.

Once you've signed up for her newsletter you're eligible to win three paperbacks. One lucky winner is picked every week. Hurry before the offer ends!

ABOUT THE AUTHOR

Dianne lives in Huntington Beach, California, with her husband, Tom, a former California State Senator, and her boxer dog, Kelly. Her passions are cooking, reading, and dogs, so whenever she has a little free time, you can either find her in the kitchen, playing with Kelly in the back yard, or curled up with the latest book she's reading. Her award-winning books include:

Cedar Bay Cozy Mystery Series

Cedar Bay Cozy Mystery Series - Boxed Set

Liz Lucas Cozy Mystery Series

Liz Lucas Cozy Mystery Series - Boxed Set

High Desert Cozy Mystery Series

High Desert Cozy Mystery Series - Boxed Set

Northwest Cozy Mystery Series

Northwest Cozy Mystery Series - Boxed Set

Midwest Cozy Mystery Series

Midwest Cozy Mystery Series - Boxed Set

Jack Trout Cozy Mystery Series

Cottonwood Springs Cozy Mystery Series

Cottonwood Springs Mystery Series – Boxed Set

Coyote Series

Midlife Journey Series, Midlife Journey Series – Boxed Set

Red Zero Series, Black Dot Series

The Holly Lewis Mystery Series, The Holly Lewis Mystery Series – Boxed Set

Newsletter

If you would like to be notified of her latest releases please go to www.dianneharman.com and sign up for her newsletter.

Website: www.dianneharman.com,
Blog: www.dianneharman.com/blog
Email: dianne@dianneharman.com

PUBLISHING 12/6/19

HOLLY & THE ORACLE

BOOK FIVE OF

THE HOLLY LEWIS MYSTERY SERIES

http://getbook.at/HTO

A charismatic Oracle who promises miracles
But only if you're willing to give money
A naïve young man who wants to belong to something
And is ready to give his hard-earned money

Convincing someone who's drinking the "Kool-Aid" that they're being taken advantage of can be difficult, but that's Holly's challenge when her friend, Levi, falls under the Oracle's spell.

Holly confronts the Oracle only to find that her friend, Levi, doesn't want her help. It never occurs to Holly that her "help" may not only result in her death, but those of her loved ones as well.

If you liked Nancy Drew, don't miss the fifth book in the Holly Lewis Mystery Series by a two-time USA Today Bestselling Author.

Open your smartphone, point and shoot at the QR code below. You will be taken to Amazon where you can pre-order 'Holly & The Oracle'.

(Download the QR code app onto your smartphone from the iTunes or Google Play store in order to read the QR code below.)